EMMY

Emmy was listed by the New York City Library
as one of its Books for the Teen Age;
the novel was also selected as
a Notable 1992 Children's Trade Book
in the Field of Social Studies.

EMMY

Connie Jordan Green

TELLICO BOOKS
Oak Ridge, Tennessee

Tellico Books is an imprint of the Iris Publishing Group, Inc

www.tellicobooks.com

Design: Robert B. Cumming, Jr.

Library of Congress Cataloging-in-Publication Data

Green, Connie Jordan.
Emmy / Connie Jordan Green. — 2nd ed.
    p. cm.
Summary: In the 1920s when her father is disabled in a coal mining
accident, eleven-year-old Emmy and the others in her family do what
they can to help, with her fourteen-year-old brother taking Pa's place in
the mines.
ISBN 978-1-60454-000-0 (pbk. : alk. paper)
[1. Coal mines and mining—Fiction. 2. Family life—Fiction. 3. Country
life—Fiction.] I. Title.
PZ7.G81925EM 2007
[Fic]—dc22
                                              2007046727

Dedicated to the memory of my uncle, William (Bill) Rockford Hall, who did for his family what Gene does for his, and to the memory of my mother, Ruth Hall Jordan, whose stories inspired this book; to Charles Curtis for sharing his knowledge of the banjo; to my writing friends for patiently critiquing this and all manuscripts; to my editors for knowing what I wanted to say; and especially to my husband, Dick, for sustaining me.

EMMY

One

THE BELL RANG AGAIN. This time the sound went on and on, the way it often did, so that Emmy felt there was no escape from it.

"Emmy Mourfield! Have you gone deaf?" Pa called from the back room.

She glanced at the clock on the kitchen shelf. Almost eleven. She was making biscuits and had to get them in the oven soon. The first boarders would be ready to eat before eleven-thirty.

"Emmy!"

"Coming, Pa." Emmy laid down the biscuit cutter and brushed flour from her hands.

"What is it, Pa?" she asked as she entered the darkened bedroom.

Pa sat on the side of the bed, his injured leg propped on a chair, his undershirt exposing the stump of his left arm. A growth of beard several days old covered his chin. "It's this here water." He sloshed the water around in a glass. "It's got so warm, it don't do a body no good to drink it."

Emmy picked up the glass. "Soon as I get the biscuits in the oven, I'll bring you some more water."

"If I ain't dead from heat or thirst by then." Pa settled back against his pillows, reaching across his body with his right hand to ease his useless leg onto the bed.

Emmy pulled open the window curtain and started to raise the window.

"What're you doing?" he asked in a querulous voice.

"Maybe if you had some air in here, you wouldn't be so hot."

"Leave that window be. I don't want any nosy neighbors looking in here."

"Pa, there isn't anybody in our backyard."

"You heard me. Leave it be. If'n I want people staring at me, I'll go to the square and sit on the steps of the company store."

Emmy pulled the curtain shut. As she left the room, Pa's voice followed her. "And I'll hang a sign around my neck. 'Look what the mines did to me,' it'll say."

In the kitchen Emmy's older brother Everett was putting two more lumps of coal into the cookstove. "Ma said to keep the fire hot. She's aiming to can beans this afternoon," he said

Emmy could scarcely breathe in the hot kitchen. But she didn't fuss at Everett. It wouldn't do any good. He couldn't help the fact that Ma had to can and had to have a hot stove to do it on. None of them—not Ma, nor Everett, nor oldest brother Gene, nor younger sister Dahlia, nor the two youngest, Kate and Marvin—could help the fact that they had to work as hard as possible to keep themselves fed now that Pa wasn't able to work.

"Where is Ma?" Emmy asked.

"She went down to the store to see if she could get credit to buy some sugar. She said all these blackberries we've been picking are a good thing, but it sure does take a lot of sugar to sweeten them into pie for the boarders."

A wail came from the back porch. "Emmy!"

"What is it, Dahlia?"

"Kate said she was tired of breaking beans, and she took Marvin and went down to the creek."

"Well, never mind about them. You just finish those beans so Ma will be able to can them after dinner."

"But it's no fair," Dahlia said. "I don't like to break beans either."

Emmy stepped to the back door. "Dahlia, I don't like to make biscuits. Everett doesn't like to build fires. Probably Gene didn't want to leave home and go cut wood for the Slones. And I bet Ma doesn't like to get up at daylight and work in the garden and cook and wash dishes and can all afternoon."

"But why do you let Kate…?"

"'Cause Kate's only six and you're all of nine and plenty big enough to do your share," Emmy said. At eleven-and-a-half, she sometimes felt years and years older than Dahlia.

Emmy went back into the kitchen, but not before she saw Dahlia's chin quivering. She knew her sister would be crying in another minute, but she didn't have time to do anything to cheer her up. Besides, she thought with a grin, maybe if she cries on the beans, Ma won't have to put much salt on them.

Everett was through stoking the fire, and he stood in the middle of the kitchen, one bare foot on top of the other. Emmy walked around him and put the pan of biscuits into the oven. She picked up a dish towel to lift the pot of potatoes from the stove.

"Here, I'll do that for you," Everett said.

"Thanks," Emmy said.

He set the pot on the table, and Emmy began mashing the soft potatoes.

"Emmy…"

She looked up.

"About this evening…"

"What about this evening?"

"Ma said when the sun drops down a little, she wants us all to go out and pick some more blackberries."

Emmy nodded. She wasn't looking forward to one more evening of picking berries. The briers were like something evil that searched out a way to get past her clothes and into her skin. She looked down at her hands. They were stained black around the nails, and the backs were pricked so that it looked as if she'd been in a fight with a cat. And the cat won, she thought.

"Well, I'm not going," Everett said.

"How're you going to get out of it?"

"That's what I need to talk to you about. You see, the Baileytown baseball team is going to be practicing, and me and Jim Bob—"

"Emmy, where's Marvin?" Ma rushed in the back door and dropped her sack of sugar on the table.

"Kate took him down to the creek," Emmy said.

Ma frowned. "I don't like those little ones off without one of you." She sighed. "But I guess they're safe enough. They probably make enough racket to scare off snakes and anything else."

She opened the oven door. Then she smiled. "You're a good girl, Emmy. Those biscuits look better'n my own."

Emmy smiled, too. It was nice to have praise from Ma. Not that Ma had ever been stingy with her praise. It was just that since Pa's accident, Ma hadn't had time to do much praising. Mostly what she did now was give orders—sweep around the table and clean off the oilcloth before the next round of boarders comes to eat; wash the dishes carefully; and dry those plates and glasses to a fare-thee-well so the boarders won't be able to complain of a single spot.

Boarders, boarders. A year ago Emmy hadn't even known there were people in the mining town who didn't live in regular houses with their families. The men and women who took meals with Emmy's family roomed at the company clubhouse or with other families in the coal town. They worked for the coal company, running the soda fountain and the store and the company offices. Many of them were unmarried, but even some of the married ones chose not to move their families to Baileytown, preferring instead to go home to their families on weekends.

Pa's bell rang again. Ma looked toward the bedroom door, the frown returning to her face. "I'm back, Frank," she called, "but I don't have time to come in right now. The first of the boarders will be here any minute."

"Just send Emmy in here," Pa called back.

Emmy looked at the glass she had set on the table. "I forgot," she said. "Pa's hot and thirsty."

"Aren't we all?" Ma said wearily, tying an apron around her waist.

Emmy scooped a dipper full of fresh water from the bucket sitting by the back door. She carried the full glass into the bedroom. "Here you are, Pa."

Pa reached out his hand that always used to be blackened by coal dust and skinned up from hard work. Now the hand was pale, and as clean and smooth as a baby's.

"Ah," he said as he tilted the glass to his mouth. Then he exclaimed, "Phew!" and spat the water across the bed. He thrust the glass back toward Emmy.

"What's wrong, Pa?" Emmy took the glass.

"I told you that water was too warm. Go up to the spring and fetch me some decent water. All of you must be trying to kill me off, now that I'm laid up and no good to anybody."

"Now, Pa, don't talk like that." Emmy turned to leave.

"I won't never be okay again," Pa muttered. "There ain't no way to grow a new arm, and a one-armed miner's no good to anyone."

"I'll bring you some cold water." Emmy hurried out of the room. She hated it when Pa talked about not getting well. Every night before she fell asleep, she prayed that Pa would be better soon. And her prayers weren't just because she and Ma and Gene and Everett and Dahlia had to work so hard. She prayed because she couldn't bear to see her once-strong father lying in bed day after day, growing more and more quarrelsome. Sometimes she found it almost impossible to love him, and on those days she prayed harder than ever.

Two

As ma dished up bowls of potatoes and beans, Everett carried them into the dining room, where the first seating of boarders was gathered around the table. Emmy filled a basket with biscuits and took it to the table.

"There's our girl," one of the men greeted her. Emmy smiled. Most of the people who ate with them were nice.

The boarders were seated at a table that used to be in the kitchen, a big table around which she and her family had eaten all their meals ever since she could remember. Last February, Ma had decided cooking was the only thing she knew how to do that other people would pay her for. Emmy, Ma, Gene, and Everett had wrestled the big table through the kitchen door and into what used to be the sitting room. They moved the sofa up against a wall and set the table near the windows. On hot summer days, like today, the breeze cooled the diners. And on cold days, the kind they had been having in late February when they started the boardinghouse, the coal fire in the grate kept the room warm while sunlight coming through the windows brightened the table.

Ever since they had brought Pa home from the hospital, Ma had slept on the sofa. It was lumpy and narrow, and Emmy thought it looked even more uncomfortable than the bed she shared with Dahlia and Kate. But Ma never complained.

Because they had only four small rooms and a lean-to in their miner's house, the sitting room had to double, for the time being anyway, as Ma's sleeping room and the dining room.

"Uh, Emmy." It was Mr. Peterson, the coal company manager for the mining town. He ate lunch with them, even though his family lived in town, in the row of houses highest on the ridge.

"Yes, Mr. Peterson. Can I get you something else?"

"No, thank you. I'd just like you to tell your ma I need to speak to her sometime in the next few days if she has time to come by my office."

Emmy frowned. "I'll tell her. There isn't anything wrong with the food, is there?"

"No, no. Best food I've ever eaten. Just tell her I'd like to talk to her."

Mr. Peterson smiled, though Emmy didn't think the smile quite reached his eyes. But he was a kind man. The coal company paid Ma twenty-five cents for each company employee's meal. Sometimes Mr. Peterson paid Ma a nickel or dime more than the twenty-five cents. He would just pat Ma on the back and say, "Anybody as big as I am is bound to eat more than his share every once in a while." But now he looked serious.

As soon as the first diners were through, Emmy, Everett, and Dahlia quickly cleared the table. Ma had set a pan of hot, soapy water on the worktable, and they scraped the few bits of food left on the plates into a pail, then dunked the plates into the water. Ma washed the plates as fast as they put them in her pan.

"One of you start drying," Ma ordered, glancing at the clock.

Dahlia picked up a towel.

"Emmy, check that fresh pan of biscuits to be sure they don't burn. Everett's got that fire hot enough to singe the tail off the devil."

"You said you wanted to can—" Everett began.

"I'm not criticizing you, son. I'm just stating the facts."

Pa's bell sounded again. "Oh!" Emmy cried. "I forgot to get Pa fresh water from the spring." She moved toward the back porch, where an empty pail stood.

"He'll just have to settle for a drink out of this bucket," Ma said, pointing to the bucket of water Everett had carried in early that morning. "I can't spare you to go to the spring right now."

"Yes, Ma," Emmy said.

The bell rang again. "Where is that Emmy?" Pa called.

Emmy looked questioningly at Ma, who shook the water off her hands, dried them on her apron, and stepped to the bedroom door. "Frank, Emmy is getting ready to serve the next boarders. Just as soon as they've eaten, I'll fix you a nice plate of food. And maybe there'll be a little cool buttermilk left."

Ma turned back to the dishes, her mouth set in a straight line.

"I could go get a little water in a pail," Dahlia said.

Ma shook her head briefly. "Not just now."

Emmy looked at Dahlia in surprise. Her sister never volunteered to do anything to help out. When they wanted Dahlia, they had to find her first, then lay down the law about whatever chore she had to do.

A call came from the sitting room. "We're here!" The next set of boarders had arrived.

"Oh, my Lord," Ma said.

For the next half hour Ma, Emmy, Everett, and Dahlia bustled about putting food on the table, refilling glasses, and, finally, clearing the table. As the last boarder left, Ma said, "Now, young'uns, let's clean this kitchen and get something to eat ourselves."

Emmy knew Ma was in a pretty good mood when she called them "young'uns." When she was angry, or too busy to be sociable, she called them each by name, starting with the oldest, as if they were hired help.

Emmy was afraid her message from Mr. Peterson would spoil Ma's mood, but she had to deliver it anyway.

"Now what do you suppose he wants?" Ma asked. "We're behind on paying the store, but Hazel gave me credit for the sugar, so I don't suppose Mr. Peterson would be concerned about that."

"Maybe he just wants you to cook fried chicken more often," Emmy said, remembering how many chicken legs Mr. Peterson usually heaped on his plate.

Ma shook her head. Emmy didn't really think Mr. Peterson wanted to talk about food either, but she was trying to think of something he'd need to discuss that wouldn't be worrisome.

When they had carried the serving bowls back to the kitchen, Emmy picked up the water buckets. "I'll go get some fresh water for Pa now," she said.

Ma looked at her quickly. "I'm not about to forget your pa. Everett, you go after water. Emmy, you better find Marvin and Kate. And Dahlia, you wash enough dishes for us to eat from."

Emmy was glad to escape the hot kitchen and happy not to have to carry the heavy water buckets back from the spring. Everett followed her across the backyard.

"I was fixing to tell you about tonight," he said.

"Yeah, blackberry picking. And you said you weren't going to help."

"Well, I didn't mean it just like that."

"What are you going to do?"

Everett swung the water buckets together, their sides colliding with a dull thud. They were made of cedar, the only material Ma felt was decent for holding drinking water. She had brought the buckets with her from her parents' farm when she married Pa and moved into the mining town.

"What I aim to do," Everett said, "is to go over to Pikesbury to the baseball game on Saturday."

"Pikesbury! How're you going to get all the way over there? And what's that got to do with tonight?"

"It's got everything to do with tonight. Me and Jim Bob have got it figured out. Petey, the team's manager, told us he'd take us to all the games if we'd do a little work—carry water for the men and do stuff like that. And I reckon I'm as good as anybody at carrying water." He swung one of the buckets in a full circle.

"You better be careful," Emmy said. "You bust one of Ma's buckets and you won't get out of the house for a year."

Everett frowned at the bucket. "Anyway, I need your help."

"What do you want me to do?"

"Me and Jim Bob have to start carrying water and chasing balls this evening at practice. I'm afraid Ma won't let me go if I ask her, so I'm not going to take any chances. I'm going to go to the blackberry patch with you and Dahlia and Kate, then I'm going to slip away."

"But if you're not back by the time we leave the blackberry patch, Ma will miss you."

"Yeah, that's where you come in."

Emmy looked at her brother. He was only a year and-a-half older than she, almost thirteen now, but he always seemed much older to her. He was willing to take chances she'd never dare to. Ma would skin her alive if she slipped out. Everett knew Ma would get mad at him if she found out. But he also knew in a day or so she'd forget he'd ever misbehaved.

Everett had inherited more than his share of Pa's love of fun. Whenever the family or the neighbors had a gathering, especially if music and dancing were a part of it, Everett was right there. His toe would tap and his eyes would shine, just the way Pa always responded to a good time. Emmy supposed it was that bit of Pa in Everett that made it so easy for Ma to forget most of Everett's devilment.

"I'm going to pick my share of the blackberries this afternoon right after we get through canning," Everett said. "Then you can bring my berries in with yours, and if Ma asks where I am, just tell her I've gone off someplace with Jim Bob. After all, that won't be a lie."

"Okay," Emmy agreed. She was relieved to hear Everett planned to pick blackberries first. It wasn't like him to shirk his part of the work. And he was right; she wouldn't be lying to Ma—as long as Ma didn't ask many questions.

Three

"Emmy, look what we made," Kate called as Emmy climbed over the rocks along the creek bank.

"Yum," Emmy said, looking at the flattened circles of mud lined up along the rocks. "Maybe we can serve your pies to the boarders tomorrow."

Kate clapped her hands, and Marvin did the same. Then he scooped up one of the mud pies, and Emmy caught him just before he put it in his mouth. "We're only teasing, Marvin," she said. "The boarders can't really eat mud, and neither can you."

But life surely would be easier if we all could, Emmy thought. Dirt was plentiful around the mining town, most of it so black with coal dust that when it was wet it looked like good, rich chocolate.

"Come on, you two. It's time to eat dinner—real dinner, I mean," she said, lifting Marvin and taking Kate by the hand.

Kate and Marvin were almost inseparable, which made keeping track of Marvin easy. He was always with Kate, and Kate was like a little mother, seeing that Marvin never got hurt. The two of them were as close as Emmy and Everett. Maybe, Emmy thought, that was what was wrong with Gene and Dahlia. They were each loners in a family of twos.

On the few occasions when Ma reminisced, she talked

about how close Gene and Belle had been, not just in age, but as playmates and companions. "Just like you and Everett," she would say to Emmy. Belle had died of scarlet fever in 1915, when she was barely six and Gene was only four-and-a-half. Emmy, who was just two years old when Belle died, had no memories of her older sister. It seemed strange even to think of Belle as her older sister. She was perpetually six, a young child represented by a small tombstone in the cemetery perched on the steep mountainside above the mining town.

All the while he was growing up, Gene kept to himself, preferring to shoot marbles in the dirt instead of hunting up some boys for a game of Dead Man or Tracers. Even now, at fourteen, he often went off into the woods for days at a time to hunt.

Dahlia had always been a loner as far as the family was concerned. The twins, who followed her by a year-and-a-half, were stillborn. But unlike Gene, Dahlia surrounded herself with friends outside the family. All as prissy as she is, Emmy thought.

By the time Emmy had gotten Kate and Marvin back to the house and washed off, Everett was there with fresh water, and Ma and Dahlia had a plate of food ready for Pa. Today, with fresh vegetables from the garden, there was plenty left over for the family, not like it had been some days in late winter and early spring when the boarders had cleaned the bowls. Then Ma would scurry around finding enough of one thing and another to fill the children's plates. She always said she was too tired to eat much herself, but Emmy noticed Ma's appetite was fine when there was food to go around.

"Why don't you let Everett help you into the kitchen, Frank, so you can eat with your young'uns?" Ma asked Pa from the doorway.

"Now, Sally, you know I'll not have people staring at me, not even people in my own house. I'll just stay right here. If any of you can spare the time to bring me some food, I'll eat it."

Ma gave up with a shrug and motioned Dahlia to take the plate in to Pa.

Every mealtime Ma went through the same thing. Emmy wondered how much longer Ma would continue to try to talk Pa into leaving the bedroom. Emmy remembered how Pa had looked sitting at the table, the skin around his eyes crinkled with laughter as he told a good story he'd heard.

She looked at the rest of the family seated around the kitchen worktable, which Gene had rigged from rough-sawn boards laid across two carpenter's horses. They were all too tired after feeding the boarders to carry their own plates into the sitting room to the proper table.

"Are those beans ready for canning this afternoon?" Ma asked Dahlia.

Dahlia sniffed and tossed her head. "Yes'm, they're ready, even if I did have to do them all by myself." She looked hard at Emmy.

Emmy just grinned at her—giving her the treatment she'd learned long ago drove her sister crazy. Dahlia loved starting an argument with Emmy, and nothing made her madder than Emmy's refusing to fight.

Ma looked at the clock. "Kate, you and Marvin go into the front bedroom, and see to it you both rest a couple of hours. Emmy and Everett, get that water boiling and sterilize those canning jars. Dahlia, help me wash all these beans and get them in another pot of boiling water. And Everett, I suppose we'll need a couple more buckets of water before long." Ma stood and stretched. "It looks like that's all the sitting we're going to have time for. Let's get to work."

Emmy went to get Pa's plate. It was still half full, but he had set it on the nightstand and was lying with his eyes closed. "Are you through, Pa?" she asked quietly.

He didn't answer.

Emmy knew he wasn't asleep; his breathing wasn't heavy enough. Even though Pa was only thirty-four, he had spent almost twenty years of his life in the coal mines. His breathing was as labored as the breathing of all the other men who had spent years digging coal underground. Emmy remembered her grandad, Pa's dad, who had slept sitting up the last ten years of his life in order to breathe. He had died at fifty when he was still going down in the mines every day.

She smoothed the sheet over Pa and took the plate back to the kitchen.

By four o'clock, when they had to start preparing the evening meal for the boarders, twenty quart-jars of green beans glowed like jewels on the windowsills where they were cooling. Emmy thought they were even more valuable than jewels; the beans would feed the boarders several meals next winter when there would be no food from the garden.

Ma laid her arm across Emmy's shoulder. "Well, young'uns, it's been an afternoon well spent. And when I saw Mrs. Bradford at the store this morning, she said her garden's got more beans than she can use with just her and Mr. Bradford home now, so, Everett, if you'll go pick tomorrow morning while the girls help me start dinner...." Ma looked around. "Where's Everett? He was right here a minute ago."

Before Ma could ask more questions, Emmy dashed out the back door with an armload of dish towels for the clothesline. She knew where Everett was—he had gone to pick his blackberries.

AFTER THE BOARDERS LEFT, the family ate their evening meal. As Emmy and Dahlia were sweeping the sitting room, someone walked onto the porch and called, "Anyone at home?"

Emmy went to the door. It was Nick Hall, Jim Bob's father and one of Pa's best friends.

"Come in, Mr. Hall," she said.

"How's your pa today?" Mr. Hall asked.

"He's about the same," Emmy said.

Mr. Hall nodded his head. "Still won't get out, huh?"

"No, sir, he won't leave his bed."

"Reckon he'll see me?"

"I'll ask him," Emmy said. Nick Hall was one of the few people, besides the doctor, whom Pa had allowed in his room since he'd been hurt.

"Tell him it's important. I've got news about the union."

Pa shook his head firmly when Emmy said he had company. But he gave in when she told him what Nick Hall had said.

"The union, you say?"

Emmy nodded. "That's what Mr. Hall said."

"Well, it's too late for me, but I reckon the union might do some other man a little good one of these days, if all I've heard is true. Come on in here, Nick," he called in a stronger voice than Emmy had heard for some time.

Nick Hall closed the door behind him. Emmy wished she could hear what the men were saying. *Union* was a word she had heard more and more during the past few years. She had looked up union in the dictionary at school last year, but the definition didn't have anything to do with miners. Still, she heard excitement in the voices of all the men when they said the word. They talked, too, about a man, John L. Lewis, who was president of the union now.

The men spoke the name in the same tone of voice they used in church. Last summer, before Pa had his accident, when he was still her jovial, outgoing pa, Emmy had asked if John L. Lewis was like Jesus. Ma had shushed her immediately.

"Don't be sacrilegious, Emmy," Ma had said.

"Now, Sally, leave the girl be," Pa had said. "Maybe she ain't being sacrilegious at all. Maybe she's speaking more truth than any of us knows."

TRUE TO HIS PROMISE, Everett walked to the berry patch with Emmy, Dahlia, and Kate. Ma said Marvin was too little to turn loose in the briers. She said that she spent more time doctoring his scratches, chiggers, and ticks than was worth it for the little handful of berries he picked. She had set him to playing on the kitchen floor while she made pie crusts for the next day.

When they got to the berry patch, Everett motioned Emmy to one side. "Here's my full bucket," he said, pulling back some briers where he'd hidden it. "It sure was hot out here before the sun went behind the mountain." Everett smiled. "But now it's all going to be worth it."

Being careful not to let Dahlia or Kate see him, Everett slipped out the far side of the berry patch. Emmy watched him hurry down the mountainside to ball practice.

When they started back home later, Dahlia asked where Everett was. "Oh, he finished early," Emmy said airily, showing Dahlia Everett's full bucket.

Dahlia looked skeptical. "Well, he sure did pick fast. I don't remember seeing him at all after we got to the patch."

Four

NEXT MORNING MA WENT OFF EARLY to see Mr. Peterson. "I might as well get it over with," she told Emmy. "It can't be anything good, or he would just have told me about it after dinner." As soon as she had prepared breakfast for the three boarders who came for that meal, Ma had made her pies. Now Emmy was cooking the remaining berries for canning.

"Blackberry pie in the winter is always a treat," Ma had said. But Emmy wondered how many of the pies the family would even get to taste this year.

Emmy figured Ma had aged at least five years in the last few months. She was carrying the entire responsibility for the family on her shoulders. In the past, Ma and Pa discussed every problem that came up, but today Ma had said, "Don't let your pa know where I've gone."

Pa's bell rang.

Emmy hurried to the bedroom door. "Yes, Pa."

"I'm thirsty again…for a fresh drink of springwater."

"Oh, Pa, I can't go right now. Ma told me to cook the berries, and if I don't keep stirring, they'll stick."

"Well, then, send one of the others."

"There's nobody here but me. Everett's picking beans at Mrs. Bradford's, and Dahlia took Kate and Marvin with her to visit her friend Priscilla Dowdy."

Pa's face softened into a smile. "I reckon me being laid up has turned you youngsters into right smart workers."

"Yes, Pa, even Marvin has learned to fetch clean dishcloths for Ma."

"My babies are growing up." Pa looked wistful for a moment. Then his face closed into the expression it had worn for the last few months. "Well, if there's nobody around to bring me water, that's just the way it is, then."

"I'm sorry, Pa," Emmy said.

She went back to the stove, stirring the berries just in time. A few had begun to stick to the bottom of the pot.

Ma came back looking more tired than when she left. She snapped out orders while she and Emmy ladled the hot berries into jars and set them in a pot of boiling water. Then she sent Emmy to get Dahlia. "That child can't be counted on. I told her to be home by ten-thirty to help with dinner."

Emmy met Dahlia, Kate, and Marvin on the road. Dahlia was smiling and showing off a new ribbon in her hair. "Priscilla gave it to me," she said proudly. "It's my birthday present, a few months late."

A handout, Emmy wanted to shout—and from the Dowdys, at that. Her neck grew hot with shame, but she only said, "Ma's in a bad mood. You'd better hurry home."

The kitchen was quiet through the rest of the dinner preparations. Emmy and Dahlia tried to anticipate Ma's needs so she wouldn't have a reason for fussing at them.

Whistling between his teeth, Everett walked up on the back porch with a bushel of beans. After one look into the kitchen, he settled quietly to the chore of breaking the beans. Emmy could imagine he was happy to have a job out of Ma's way.

Finally dinner was on the table. Mr. Peterson came in with the other boarders and took his seat. He asked for more food when his plate was empty, but otherwise he didn't say anything.

After the second seating of boarders had left, Ma sank into a chair. She stared straight ahead, not moving out of the way as Emmy, Everett, and Dahlia carried the dishes into the kitchen, and not offering to help scrape or wash.

They worked until the kitchen was orderly enough that they could eat their own dinner. Ma had still not moved. Kate and Marvin were beginning to whine, so Dahlia fixed some food for them and took them out to the backyard.

"Ma," Emmy said, "can I get you something to eat?"

Ma rubbed a hand over her forehead. Then she slowly looked up at Emmy. "We're about to be evicted," she said.

"Ma!" Emmy said. "They can't do that."

"I'm afraid they can. The company's rule is that these houses are only for families of miners. That's what Mr. Peterson had to tell me."

"But it's the coal company's fault Pa can't work anymore. He got hurt in *their* mines. They can't just throw us out." Emmy felt anger rising in her the way the heat had risen in the pot of berries earlier that day, pushing its way up until her blood threatened to boil like the berries.

Everett clenched his fists. "I'll go talk to Mr. Hall. Jim Bob said his pa and some other men were talking to those union organizers over at—"

"Everett," Ma said sharply, "we'll keep our troubles to ourselves."

"Well, I reckon when we're sitting on the side of the road with all our belongings, folks will know about our troubles." He started out of the room.

"You come right back in here," Ma ordered. Everett sat in the nearest chair, his head lowered.

"I've been studying on this the last few hours. I want you

to go over to Hawkins Branch this afternoon and get your brother Gene. The only way we can keep this house is if we have someone working in the mines. I guess Gene's going to have to go load coal." Ma stood up, her back straight and her chin in the air.

Emmy and Everett looked at each other. After Pa's accident, Ma had said no member of her family was ever again going down in the mines. Gene had friends who had quit school and gone into the mines, but Ma and Pa had insisted Gene stay in school. This summer he had gone to Mr. Slone's to help with the saw milling, and he was to go back to school in the fall.

And now Ma had changed her mind. She must be desperate, Emmy thought, but what's Pa going to say?

Emmy walked to the edge of town with Everett, who carried Pa's old lunch pail with two pieces of chicken and some biscuits in it. He would be late getting back home.

"Go tell Jim Bob I can't make it tonight," he said to Emmy. "Tell him something came up, but I'll be there tomorrow night. Make him understand I aim to be the other water boy for the team. I don't want him finding somebody to take my place."

Emmy watched Everett disappear down the dusty road. She would have liked to be the one going after Gene, spending the next two hours walking along the road, the tall mountains rising on either side. She and Everett knew where several springs were between Baileytown and Hawkins Branch, and she thought about lying beside one of the springs, her hair dangling into the water, the cool air rising around her face.

Back when Pa worked and they had time for such things, the family sometimes walked on Sunday afternoons to visit cousins in the surrounding towns. They only knew cousins on Pa's side of the family. Ma's family lived in the other direction, miles and miles away where the land flattened out enough for a family to live off their farming. Except for getting a faraway look on her face when she rubbed her hands over the wooden water buckets, Ma acted as if she had never had any family except Pa and Gene, Everett, Emmy, Dahlia, Kate, and Marvin. And the three little ones up in the cemetery.

But it was Everett setting out on the road, not Emmy. Ma couldn't spare two of her children for the afternoon, and she wouldn't let Emmy go alone. "There's too much devilment around these mining towns for a young girl to be out by herself," she had said. Then she had looked Emmy up and down. "You'll soon be twelve and coming on to the time when you're a young lady. We have to be careful with you."

Emmy sometimes looked into the piece of mirror hanging above the washstand on the back porch, the spot where Pa used to shave. She couldn't tell any difference in the way she looked now and the way she'd looked for the past few years, except maybe her arms seemed longer than ever and her face was even thinner than it used to be. If she was coming on to being a young lady, it was obvious only to Ma.

When she reached the Halls' house, Jim Bob was sitting on his porch, some pieces of wire and part of an old wooden box beside him. "Come on in," he called. "Where's Everett?"

Emmy gave him Everett's message, not mentioning the family's troubles.

"Well, shoot, why would I want to get somebody else?" Jim Bob asked. "Me and Everett have been buddies since we was little. Look what I'm doing," he said, pointing to the pile of materials.

Emmy nodded.

"You know what that is?"

"It looks like a box without a top."

"Well, it is right now. But it's going to be a turtle trap."

"A turtle trap?"

"Yeah, when I get this finished, me and Everett are going to take this down to the creek and put it on the bottom. We're going to catch that big snapping turtle we've seen in the water."

"What do you want with a snapping turtle?"

"We'll eat him—Ma makes good turtle soup—and then we'll sell his shell. There's a man over in Pikesbury that makes all sorts of things out of turtle shells. I bet he'll pay me and Everett a pretty penny for a shell that big."

Jim Bob and Everett were a good pair, Emmy thought as she walked home. What one of them didn't think up, the other did.

Five

Emmy was getting into bed when she heard Gene and Everett come into the house. She crept to the door opening onto the sitting room, leaving Dahlia and Kate asleep in the bed. Marvin lay on his cot, curled into a ball, sleeping as hard as he had played all day.

Ma was waiting up for her sons. "You're a sight for sore eyes," she said, hugging Gene. "Hattie Slone must have fed you well. You look like you've grown a foot."

"Ma," Gene said with a laugh, "I've only been gone two months." Then he grew sober. "Everett told me about our trouble. I'll go to the mines tomorrow and see if I can get on."

Ma nodded and patted his shoulder.

Pa coughed in the next room. "What's going on out there?" he called.

Ma, Gene, and Everett looked at one another. Then Gene stepped forward. "It's me, Pa. I've come back home."

"Go on in and see him," Ma whispered to Gene. "But don't mention about the mines."

Emmy moved to the door that led from the front bedroom into Pa's room. The door was closed, but by standing close to it, she could hear through the keyhole everything that was said. As long as she didn't actually stoop down and peer through the keyhole, she didn't feel as if she were snooping.

"It's good to see you, Pa," Gene said. "Are you getting better?"

Pa didn't bother to answer Gene's question. "Didn't they like your work over at the Slones'?" he asked.

"Yeah, they told me I was a good worker. Old Man Slone said I was about the best fourteen-year-old he'd ever seen with a peavey."

"You have to be careful. Even with the peavey hook, those big logs can get away from you," Pa commented.

"And he told me I could handle my end of a crosscut saw like a man."

"Then if they think so much of you, why'd they let you go?"

Emmy stepped even closer to the door. She didn't have to see Gene's face to know how he looked. He always burned with shame when he had to tell a lie. But it was dark now, and Pa wouldn't be able to see Gene clearly.

"They didn't exactly let me go. I just told them Ma needed me at home for a while."

"What does your ma need with you? She's got Everett and Emmy, and I reckon that's enough help for any woman."

"Well, Pa...There's just some things I can help her with that Everett and Emmy ain't big enough to do yet."

"Humph," Pa said. "Seems to me bringing a little money into the house would be the thing Ma needs most help with. Lord knows I'm not ever again going to be good for anything except to lie in bed and be a burden."

"Now, Pa, don't talk like that. You know you're not a burden to any of us."

Emmy heard Gene move across the floorboards to stand next to Pa's bed.

"I reckon if you've taken care of us for all these years, the least I can do is help take care of you now," Gene said.

Emmy felt a lump form in her throat, and she backed

away from the door and crawled into bed. She snuggled in next to Kate and rolled her toward the center of the bed. Because she was the youngest, Kate had to sleep in the middle. She didn't seem to mind, but Emmy would have hated to be hemmed in by two other people, to face someone no matter which way she turned.

NEXT MORNING EMMY woke to the smell of frying bacon. Gene was sitting at the kitchen table, and Ma was cooking breakfast.

Emmy sat on the bench next to Gene.

"What're you doing up so early?" he asked, tousling her hair.

Emmy smoothed her hair behind her ears. But Gene just smiled at her and she smiled back.

"I guess Emmy's got some farm blood from my family," Ma said. "She can't stand to let a rooster get ahead of her." She set a plate of eggs, bacon, biscuits, and gravy in front of Gene.

"Thanks," Gene said. "As soon as I eat, I'll get over to the mining office."

"I sure hope they're hiring," Ma said.

Gene nodded. "I've heard they're digging a lot of coal. Some company men stopped over at the Slones' one night. They were looking to get an order of lumber. Said they were aiming to put up another house or two here in town."

"Well, I hope they put up their houses and don't kick us out of ours." Ma cracked another egg into the skillet. "I've been thinking about all those lumber scraps the Slones have. Do you think there'd be any way to get hold of some of them?"

"I reckon they'd let me have whatever slabs I wanted to carry off. What you got in mind?"

Ma looked at the basket of eggs beside the stove. "These

eggs are expensive, and chickens aren't hardly any trouble. I've been studying on keeping a few hens in the back, but I need a safe house to lock them in at night."

"I'll help you feed the hens, Ma," Emmy said. She thought about having a backyard full of fluffy hens cackling and scratching after worms. Last summer Mrs. Bradford had kept hens, and Emmy had gone up to her house as often as she could just to sit and watch the hens. She had always wanted a pet, but even when Pa was working, Ma had said they couldn't afford to feed any more mouths, not even the little mouth on an animal.

Gene stood up. "I better get on." He looked toward Pa's door. "I don't want Pa to wake up and ask me where I'm going."

Ma slid the egg onto a plate and set it before Emmy. Emmy had been hungry when she woke up. But now, even with a freshly cooked egg sitting in front of her, her appetite fled. All she could think about was Pa's accident, the timbers falling in on him, the light in his carbon lamp being extinguished, and the blackness swallowing him. She looked at Gene, who was heading for the mining offices, hoping to go down the long shaft that led underground to the tunnels where the men worked ten and twelve hours without seeing the light of day. She wanted to grab his arm and hold him there in the kitchen where it was bright and safe.

He went out the back door, and she heard him go down the steps.

"Eat your egg," Ma said, "before it gets cold."

When Gene had not returned by dinnertime, Ma said to Emmy, "That means they've put him straight to work. The house will be in his name, and we won't have to move."

Emmy carried Pa's plate in to him.

"Tell Gene, when he finishes eating his dinner, to come in here and talk to me. I'm aiming to find out what's going on around the hollows."

"Gene isn't here right now, Pa."

"What's your ma got him doing so soon?"

Emmy looked at her hands to keep from meeting Pa's eyes. She was no better at lying than Gene was. "I'm not sure what he's doing. He just went out early today and hasn't come back."

She felt Pa gazing at her. But then he started to eat. He smiled suddenly. "You reckon your ma's got a mind to feed us so many vegetables that when we go outside the bugs'll jump on us and leave her garden alone?"

Emmy laughed. It was the first time in months Pa had wisecracked the way he used to do.

A part of Emmy wanted to stay and talk to Pa while he was in a good mood, but another part of her wanted to escape the room before he asked her any more questions.

After the dishes were done, Ma gave everyone the afternoon off. "We've caught up for a day or two on canning, and it's much too hot to pick more blackberries until this evening."

"Oh, good," Dahlia said. "I'm going over to Priscilla's."

"You'll have to take Kate and Marvin with you," Ma said. "I'm going to mop the floors, and they'll be underfoot."

"Can't Emmy take care of them this time? I had to take them this morning, and Priscilla and me couldn't talk."

Ma looked at Emmy.

"Okay," Emmy said. She didn't particularly like to help Dahlia out, but she didn't want Kate and Marvin to feel they were a burden on anybody.

Dahlia put her new ribbon in her hair and skipped out the door.

"Be back by supper time," Ma called. She turned to Emmy. "Don't you want to go to Dowdy's with Dahlia? You could take Kate and Marvin along. It'd give you a chance to visit with Tennie awhile."

"It'll be cooler down by the creek," Emmy said. She had

no intention of spending her one afternoon free of chores with Tennie Dowdy. If anybody was sillier than Dahlia and Priscilla, it was Priscilla's big sister, Tennie. Tennie was two years older than Emmy, but they shared the same classroom in the small school. Still, that didn't make them friends. Tennie hung out with girls who had enough money to buy new dresses and shoes and who ate sandwiches made with white bread. Even when Pa was working, Emmy carried biscuits or a cold sweet potato for her lunch.

Near the end of the school year, when Ma needed help feeding the boarders, Emmy had left school at midmorning and just returned for the last few hours of classes.

Tennie told her one day that she was never going to amount to anything if she didn't get an education. "And it doesn't look like your parents care whether you know anything or not," Tennie had said.

Emmy wanted to reply that she could learn as much in half a day as some people learned in a full day. But Tennie was not only prissy and well dressed; she was also smart. Each Monday the class was given a verse to memorize. Tennie always knew it by the middle of the week. She stood up and recited it while everyone else was just learning the first few lines. Emmy was often with the group saying the verse at the last possible moment on Friday afternoon. Tennie sat through the recitations with her eyebrows arched and her head slightly tilted. The minute anyone confused a word or line, her hand shot up to let the teacher know there was a mistake.

Emmy didn't ever want to be like Tennie, but she did sometimes think it unfair that Tennie had so much of all the things that showed.

Six

Emmy settled Kate and Marvin on a big rock beside the creek. She filled a tin can with water and scraped loose enough dirt to keep them busy making mud pies. Then she dangled her bare feet in the creek, enjoying the cool water flowing over her dusty toes. Now that it was summer, she hardly ever wore shoes, except when she went into the berry patch.

After a few minutes she stepped into the creek, looking for places where the water would come to her knees. She pulled up her dress and tucked the skirt under her sash. The water rose around her thighs as she waded deeper. She thought how good it would feel to sit in that cool water. She looked around. Only Kate and Marvin were in sight, busily making mud pies.

Emmy waded to a large rock. She untied her sash, took off her dress, and laid the two garments on the rock. She stood there in only her underpants, the sun through the leaves making dappled shadows on her bare chest. With no shape yet to her chest, no matter what Ma said, she thought she looked like a boy. And she knew her brothers swam naked all the time.

She started to take off her underpants, but the idea was so daring it made her laugh out loud.

Kate and Marvin looked at her, then went back to making their pies.

Still wearing her underpants, Emmy waded back to the deep pool and sat on the bottom. This time the water came up around her neck. She leaned her head back so the water closed around her head like a tight-fitting cap. No, she thought, the water isn't like a cap. It feels more like Ma's fingers massaging my head while she washed my hair when I was little.

Emmy wasn't exactly swimming; she'd never learned how because Ma and Pa thought girls shouldn't be so immodest as to bathe in public. Now she felt as if she belonged in this spot and as if the rest of the world—with its hungry boarders and its deep mine shafts—didn't exist at all.

Maybe I'll just stay through supper, she thought, and through berry-picking time, and through ...

"Hey, Emmy, what do you think you're doing?"

Emmy jerked her head upright.

Jim Bob made his way down the rocks along the bank.

Emmy clutched her arms around her chest and stayed underwater. "You get away from here, Jim Bob," she called.

"How come? Everett told me to meet him here. We're about ready to try out our trap."

Everett was coming, too. But that was okay. He wouldn't tell Ma about her going in the water.

But Jim Bob...She couldn't get out of the water in her underpants with him standing there.

Jim Bob took another step toward the water. "I never knew you liked to swim, Emmy," he said. "You got a bathing costume on?"

"You stay where you are, Jim Bob."

"Ha. You're swimming naked, aren't you?" Jim Bob was at the edge of the creek now. He rolled up the legs of his overalls.

"What are you doing?" Emmy asked.

"I'm just going to wade out there and be sure you don't drown."

"You come any nearer and I'm going to scream!" Emmy cried.

"Sure you are. Then your ma will come down here and tan your hide for going swimming."

Emmy looked at her clothes on the rock. She could stay underwater until she reached the edge of the pool, but the water was only a few inches deep around the rock.

Jim Bob had waded up to his shins.

Emmy moved to the far edge of the pool.

Jim Bob took another step, and the water reached the roll of pants at his knee. "This is a good pool," he said. "Any turtles in there with you?"

"No. You're getting your pants wet. What's your ma going to say?" He was only a couple of feet away now. Emmy wasn't afraid of Jim Bob; she knew he wasn't going to hurt her. He just wanted to aggravate her, the way he had done all his life. But if he saw her without her dress, he'd tease her forever. And someday he'd forget and say something about it in front of Ma, and then Emmy would be in for it.

Jim Bob laughed. "My pants will be dry before Ma sees me."

Suddenly Emmy sprang from the water, skimming her arm across the surface, sending a spray of water straight into Jim Bob's face. She didn't stop to see if she'd hit her target, but ran to the rock and pulled her dress over her wet body. It stuck to her chest and then around her waist, but she had her back turned to Jim Bob, and wiggled until the dress fell into place.

"There," she said, turning with a triumphant smile.

Jim Bob was sitting in the pool, laughing. "I reckon since you got me wet, I might as well cool down," he said.

Emmy wanted to ask him if he'd seen her bare chest and back and her underpants, but she knew he'd say yes whether he had or not. Better to make him think she knew he hadn't seen her. But had he? And someday would he tell everyone?

Her dress was almost as wet as her underpants now. It clung to her skin and felt sticky and tight. She no longer felt as cool as she had a few minutes earlier in the silky water. That Jim Bob—he had ruined her afternoon.

Everett came bounding down the creek bank as Emmy made her way over the rocks to Kate and Marvin. The two youngsters had paid no attention to Emmy's swim nor to Jim Bob's arrival. Kate had broken up a stick and stuck the pieces in one of her mud pies.

"Look, Emmy, I made Marvin another birthday cake," Kate said. For Marvin's third birthday in May, Mr. Peterson had one of the women in town bake a special cake. He'd brought it in at dinnertime, and Ma had held Marvin up so he could blow out the three candles. Mr. Peterson cut tiny pieces for the boarders, leaving enough for all the family to have a big piece. And there was even a little left for that evening, so Marvin's birthday celebration lasted all day.

Everett laughed when he saw Jim Bob. He stripped out of his overalls and jumped into the water beside him. "Hey," he said, "how come you're swimming in your clothes?"

"I thought that was how the Mourfield family did it," Jim Bob said, looking toward Emmy.

"Naw," said Everett, "that wouldn't be any fun at all."

ONCE MORE EVERETT PICKED his share of berries in late afternoon and left the filled bucket where Emmy could find it and bring it back home with hers. This time as they left the berry patch, Dahlia looked straight at Emmy. "I know something is going on," Dahlia said. "I looked for Everett ten minutes after we got to the patch, but I couldn't find him."

Emmy just smiled. "How do you know he didn't find a better patch to pick?"

"Because," Dahlia said with a toss of her head, "I saw that bucket of berries under the briers." She pointed to Emmy's second pail. "Now you better tell me. Where did Everett go?"

"Wouldn't you like to know. Wouldn't you just like to know."

"I bet if I tell Ma, she won't have any trouble finding out what Everett's up to."

Emmy recognized a bluff when she heard one. Dahlia might tell all the world what she, Emmy, was up to, but she wouldn't tell on Everett unless she had a lot to gain from the telling. Everett was the easygoing one in the family, the one who always had a smile and whom everyone liked. Telling on Everett always made the teller end up looking extra bad.

Still, it wouldn't hurt to warn him that Dahlia was on to his evening disappearances.

Seven

GENE WAS HOME WHEN THE GIRLS GOT BACK. He and Ma sat on the front porch in two old rockers, the way Ma and Pa used to do on hot summer evenings, looking for a breeze to cool them off before bedtime. Dahlia and Kate set their buckets down and ran to Gene. He pulled Kate onto his lap and put an arm around Dahlia.

"What are you doing home, Gene?" Dahlia asked. "I thought you were going to stay in Hawkins Branch all summer."

Gene looked uncomfortable, and Emmy wondered if he would lie to the girls. If Pa wasn't to know Gene was working in the mines, it wouldn't do to tell the girls. Kate would sure enough slip and say something, not knowing any better. And who knew about Dahlia?

"I just thought I might be useful around here," he said.

"Oh, good," Dahlia said. "You can help us pick berries tomorrow night."

"Leave your brother be," Ma said. "He's tired tonight. And I reckon you three girls and Everett can pick as many berries as a body can use up before they spoil." Ma looked around. "Where is Everett, anyway?"

Dahlia looked at Emmy.

Emmy crossed the porch so her back was to Ma. "He and

Jim Bob are up to something. But see, he finished picking his share of the berries before he went off."

She went through the house and set the buckets on the back porch where they would stay cool until morning. It was too dark to wash the berries now, and Ma didn't like to light the oil lamp unless they had to have it. Besides, the lamp would give off heat, something they didn't need a bit more of this evening. And it would attract every moth around.

Kate had followed Emmy, so Emmy dipped a little water from the water bucket into a washbasin and helped Kate wipe the perspiration and berry stains from her face. Then she seated her on the back steps with the basin so she could wash her feet. A full bath in a tub was something most of the family took only once a week. In between, washings from a basin did fine. But Ma insisted everyone wash his or her feet before going to bed.

Emmy saw the damp area on the back wall below where the washtub hung. As Pa had done for years, Gene would have had a full bath after his day in the mines. Emmy wondered if Ma had carried water for him. And she wondered how they had managed the bath without Pa hearing. Gene couldn't have taken it in the kitchen, where they usually bathed. Maybe he had bathed out in the backyard.

Later, when everyone else was in bed, Emmy sat on the back steps waiting for Everett. Ma called to her that it was time to go to bed, but Emmy said she needed to cool off some more. That was certainly at least half of the truth.

"Well, I need sleep even more than I need cooling," Ma said. And she added, "What do you suppose Everett and Jim Bob are up to this late?"

Emmy didn't answer. She sat quietly, listening to jar flies singing from the trees while the breeze dried the fringe of hair next to her face. The evening had the peculiar smell of midsummer, the smell of mint growing along the creek and Ma's cosmos blooming at the edge of the garden. Even with all the planting and taking care of the garden necessary to produce enough food for the family and the boarders, Ma had still found time and room to plant flowers. "If a body can't have something pretty to look at while she works, there wouldn't be much pleasure in gardening," she said.

A low whistle from across the backyards caused Emmy to sit up straight and peer into the darkness. The sound could have been a bird, but more than likely it was Everett, not taking any chances of walking past the sitting room. He and Jim Bob were saying their own special kind of good-night.

In another minute Everett slipped through a wide place in the privet hedge.

"It's me," Emmy called softly, not wanting him to bump into her and let out a yell.

Everett sat down beside her and wiped his forehead with the tail of his shirt. "How come you're still up?" he asked.

"I wanted to warn you. Dahlia knows you're slipping off in the evenings."

"Is she going to tell?"

Emmy thought a minute. Dahlia wasn't likely to tell on Everett. Still, if she knew something, she'd somehow turn it to her good. She shrugged. "Who knows."

"I won't worry about it then." Everett stood and stretched. "Think I'll get to bed."

After waiting up for him, Emmy wasn't willing to let Everett go off to bed so fast. "Tell me about ball practice," she said.

She knew a little about baseball. Like most of the miners, Pa was a baseball fan and had played on the team when he was younger. He'd never missed a home game, and the family had usually gone with him. Emmy had never paid much attention to what was happening on the diamond, but she always liked the excitement of the crowd and the way people who ordinarily wouldn't say a cross word yelled at the umpire.

Everett sat back down. "We've got some good hitters. You ought to see…"

Emmy only half paid attention to the details Everett told her. She enjoyed sitting there in the cool of the evening, the house quiet behind her. She and Everett spoke in whispers, not wanting Ma to hear them and especially not wanting to disturb Gene, who was asleep in the lean-to he and Everett shared off the back porch.

"Why don't you go to practice with me sometime?" Everett asked. "You could sit on the side. Lots of people come to watch."

"Maybe I will," she said, and laughed softly. Today she'd gone swimming almost naked; some evening she'd slip out with Everett….Did she dare?

Next morning, Saturday, Gene left for the mines early, before Pa was awake. "Where's Gene?" Dahlia asked a few hours later as she, Ma, and Emmy sat around the table peeling potatoes. "How come he isn't helping us?"

"He's helping another way," Ma said.

"What's he doing?" Dahlia asked.

"Something none of the rest of us can do," Ma said, clamping her lips shut so that Dahlia could see that was the last word on the subject.

Emmy didn't meet Dahlia's eyes. If Dahlia suspected the rest of them were keeping something from her….

In early afternoon Everett slipped away to join Jim Bob and the team for the trip to Pikesbury. Again, Emmy was the only one who knew where he was going. Because Ma didn't need his help for the few boarders they fed on the weekends, she hardly noticed his absence.

All afternoon Emmy thought about going to practice

with Everett, but she couldn't figure out how they would manage it without Ma knowing. It was easy enough for Everett to pick his berries and for her to carry them home and cover for him. But who would carry home two extra pails? And even if Dahlia could be trusted and would agree to cover for both of them, what would Ma say if Dahlia told her Emmy had gone off with Jim Bob and Everett? Emmy was sure Ma wouldn't mind Everett helping out the team, if he'd just tell her. But Ma would never hold with a young girl going to baseball practice.

The next week Everett went to practice each evening and urged Emmy to join him. On Friday, although she still hadn't figured out how to manage the blackberry picking, Emmy made up her mind to go with him.

When the afternoon canning was finished, Dahlia went to visit Priscilla for a while. Emmy went to the creek with Everett and Jim Bob, who were ready to test their turtle trap. They placed the box on the bottom of the deep pool where Emmy had cooled off the week before.

"You mean that's where the snapping turtle lives?" Emmy asked.

Jim Bob laughed. "Yeah. You're just lucky…"

Emmy frowned at him and nodded toward Everett, who had waded into the pool and was propping open the trap.

Jim Bob winked. "…you don't like to swim," he finished. But Emmy heard him whisper under his breath, "And lucky the turtle didn't take a liking to girls in their underpants."

So he *had* seen her when she leaped out of the water. Thank heaven she hadn't decided to bathe naked!

"Now, let's go up on the bank and wait," Everett said.

The three of them sat quietly so they wouldn't alert the turtle. After a few minutes, black clouds rolled over the peak of the mountains, blocking out the sun. A cool breeze sprang up.

"Heck," Everett said, "it's going to rain out the practice."

"And blackberry picking," Emmy added.

"That would be a good thing. Then I won't have to leave in a minute to pick my share."

When the first raindrops fell, Jim Bob and Everett pulled the trap out of the water. In the mountains a shower sometimes caused flash floods, washing away everything in the creeks and alongside, and they didn't want to lose that trap.

Jim Bob sprinted home, and Emmy and Everett ran for their house. They got inside the back door just as the rain began.

Ma was scrubbing new potatoes, getting them ready to cook for tomorrow's dinner. "You just made it," she said. "I guess Dahlia is going to have to stay at Priscilla's until this is over."

And wouldn't Dahlia like it if she had to stay forever at Priscilla's, Emmy thought. Because Mr. Dowdy was mine foreman, the family lived in one of the larger mining houses, up the mountain where breezes always blew in the summer and where coal dust from the mines didn't reach. The Dowdys' house wasn't quite as high up nor as grand as those on Silk Stocking Row, the name the miners gave the large houses where the mining executives, engineers, and accountants lived—that is, where the ones who chose to bring their families to the mining towns lived.

Eight

THE RAIN BEAT AGAINST THE WINDOWS and pattered off the tin roof. Streaks of lightning lit up the kitchen. Emmy liked being safely inside during a storm, but Kate was frightened. She clung to Ma's waist and cried. Then Marvin began crying, too.

Ma pulled Kate and Marvin into her lap. "Well, now," she said, "that lightning is dancing around all over out there, but it's not going to come in our house. You're safe as can be in here."

Kate sniffled and wiped her eyes with the back of her hand. Lightning flashed once more at the window and a clap of thunder followed. Emmy jumped, and Kate burst into tears again.

Ma looked at Emmy over Kate's head. "Would you see what you can do to entertain them? Take them where they can't see all this," Ma said, nodding toward the window.

Emmy took Kate's and Marvin's hands. "Let's check on Pa."

They looked into the bedroom. Pa sat propped against the pillows, the sheet pulled over his injured leg, the empty sleeve of his shirt pinned shut. With the curtains closed, the room was dark and gloomy, the lightning an occasional glow at the window.

"Do you mind if we come in?" Emmy asked. "Kate and Marvin don't like the storm."

Pa smiled—one of his rare smiles these days. "I reckon I could stand you young'uns for a little bit."

Kate and Marvin stood shyly beside Emmy, each clinging to one of her hands. Pa had become almost like a stranger to the younger children. Emmy squeezed their hands and pulled them a little closer to the bed.

Pa moved over to the far side of the bed and tucked the sheet around his leg. He patted the half-bed he had left vacant. "Climb up here," he said.

Emmy nodded to them and helped them up onto the edge of the bed. She smiled. They looked as if they felt the way she did when she had to go see old Dr. Circle for a badly stubbed toe or a cold that wouldn't respond to Ma's mustard plasters.

She sat on the floor, cross-legged. The air was close and heavy in the room, and thunder rumbled outside. "Pa, tell us a story, maybe about when you were little."

Pa rubbed his chin. "Well, now, it wouldn't do to repeat the things I did when I was little to these tads. Might give them some ideas your ma would never be able to get out of their heads again."

"Then sing us a song."

Pa had a good voice. He used to play his banjo and sing on Saturday evenings after everyone had bathed. Sometimes they would all dance, and then Ma would fuss at Pa for getting the children so excited and hot that they were going to need another bath. But she always smiled while she fussed, and Pa would tap his foot and go into a really fast song, like "Turkey in the Straw." After that he'd wink at Ma and play a slow old ballad, and everyone would sit quietly until he was through. Then they would all go off to bed. Emmy remembered how peacefully she had slept, the sound of Pa's voice staying in her head all night.

"A song?" Pa looked worried. "It's been a long time....I ain't right sure my voice...."

Kate clapped her hands. "Sing a good one, Pa. Sing 'Barbara Allen.'"

Marvin laughed and clapped, too.

Pa sat up a little straighter. "Well, I reckon nobody would forget the words to 'Barbara Allen.' But, Emmy girl, maybe you better sing with me, just in case my voice has rusted."

Emmy nodded, and Pa began:

> *In Scarlet town, where I was born,*
> *There was a fair maid dwelling,*
> *Made every youth cry "Well away!"*

Emmy joined in on the next line:

> *Her name was Barbara Allen.*

Together they sang the second verse:

> *All in the merry month of May,*
> *When green buds they are swelling,*
> *Young Jimmy Green on his death bed lay*
> *For the love of Barbara Allen.*

Ma came to the doorway, looked at them for a moment, then stepped into the room and leaned against the wardrobe. On the next verse, she sang with Pa and Emmy:

> *He sent his man unto her there,*
> *To the town where she was dwelling;*

> *"O you must come to my master dear,*
> *If your name be Barbara Allen."*

Everett joined Ma in the doorway. He didn't sing very often. Everett lived in a family of singers, but he couldn't carry a tune. Now he tapped his toe slowly to the beat of the mournful ballad.

By the time they reached the last verse,

> *"Farewell, ye virgins all," she said,*
> *"And shun the fault I've fell in;*
> *Henceforward take warning by the fall*
> *Of cruel Barbara Allen,"*

Ma had tears in her eyes. Emmy knew happiness about Pa's singing brought Ma's tears, not pity for Barbara Allen. Ma usually nodded triumphantly at the end of the ballad. "That's what happens," she would say, looking at her children, her voice carrying a warning, "when somebody disregards the feelings of the ones that love them best."

Today all but two of the ones Ma loved best were gathered in the small, stuffy room, singing together while the storm outside moved slowly away from the mountain.

"Sing another one, Pa," Kate said.

"Another one," Marvin echoed, clapping his hands.

Pa laid his head back on the pillow and closed his eyes.

"That's enough," Ma said. "Your pa is tired now."

Pa sat up. "Now, woman, I guess I've got more than one song left in me. What would you like to hear?"

"I know," Kate said. "Play your banjo."

"Kate..." Ma began. Then she stopped and looked at Pa.

"My banjo?" Pa's voice was soft. He looked down at his right hand and flexed his fingers. "My banjo," he said again.

"I reckon my fingers remember how to pluck. But this"—he turned his gaze to the stump of his left arm—"this ain't no good for chording. Nor for any other earthly use." He closed his eyes again and pulled the sheet up to his chin.

Ma waited for a moment, then went quietly back into the kitchen.

Emmy picked up Marvin and took Kate's hand. "Come on," she said, "the storm is over."

"But I want to stay with Pa," Kate said. "I want to hear another song."

"Pa's tired," Emmy said.

"But he said…." Kate began to protest.

Emmy, still carrying Marvin, pulled Kate out of the room. "We'll make some paper dolls," Emmy said.

Kate brightened and went willingly into the kitchen. The storm had settled into a steady rain, no longer filled with flashes of lightning. But the uneasiness of the outdoors seemed to have moved indoors. Ma, who had sung from the doorway a moment ago, was now back to her overworked self, scrubbing potatoes and keeping one eye on the clock.

Emmy went to the back porch and took a newspaper from a small stack they carefully hoarded. Before the accident, Pa read the paper almost every evening, buying one whenever he felt the few pennies wouldn't be missed. But after his accident, he had shut out the world beyond the coal-mining town. For a few weeks after his return from the hospital, Ma had walked down to the company soda fountain and brought home the newspaper for Pa. But he had refused to even look at the headlines, and she had given up. Because she didn't have time during daylight hours to stop and read and because she wouldn't light the lamp at night just for her own use, Ma stopped buying the paper altogether.

In the winter, the family used newspapers to cover up drafty places in the walls, tacking the papers wherever the wind found a hole. Sometimes they used papers to start the fire, although they tried never to let the fire go out in the winter. However, on the few summer days when Ma didn't need to can and had enough cooked for supper, she would allow the fire to die in the afternoon. Then early the next morning she'd wad papers into the stove and add a few sticks of kindling to start up a new fire quickly.

There were only a few papers left. The one Emmy picked up had a December date. Despite the low supply, she felt that keeping Kate and Marvin out of Ma's hair for the afternoon was worth the sacrifice of a newspaper. With Kate and Marvin beside her at the kitchen table, she folded the paper into sections. Then she got Ma's sewing scissors. "Do you want boy or girl dolls?" she asked.

"Girls," Kate said firmly, "with big skirts."

Emmy began to cut slowly but skillfully.

"Will she have pretty slippers?" Kate asked.

"The prettiest slippers ever," Emmy answered.

"Like Cinderella's?"

"Even prettier. These are not only glass, but they have rubies and diamonds on them."

Kate sighed contentedly. Outside the rain had stopped, and the sky was turning the peculiar shade of green that follows summer rains.

Emmy was unfolding the dolls—a string of gowned ladies holding hands—when Dahlia burst through the back door. Her hair was a wet mess; the ribbon she'd been so proud of was wadded up in her hand. Her face was streaked with tears. She looked at Emmy, Kate, and Marvin, at Ma, and at Everett adjusting his turtle trap in the corner.

"I hate all of you," she cried. She hid her face in her hands while she sobbed and sobbed.

Nine

EMMY CAREFULLY PLACED THE STRING of dolls on the table. The only sound in the room was Dahlia's sobbing.

Ma dried her hands and walked over to Dahlia. She put her arm around Dahlia's shoulders. "All right, now. Tell us what this is all about."

Dahlia made an effort to stop crying.

Ma handed her a damp towel. "Wipe your face," she said gently.

Dahlia obeyed.

"What's got you so upset?" Ma asked.

"It was Tennie," Dahlia said. "She told Priscilla not to let me come to their house anymore." Dahlia sniffed hard but went on with her story. "It's all Gene's fault," she said.

"What're you talking about?" Emmy demanded.

Dahlia looked at her sister with tear-filled eyes. "You knew about it and you didn't tell me. All of you knew, and now I don't have any friends left." This time Dahlia couldn't stop the tears from streaming down her face.

"You're not making any sense, Dahlia," Emmy said.

Ma motioned for Emmy to be quiet. "Now just calm down, child," she said to Dahlia. "Whatever is going on won't get any better until you tell us all about it."

"Yes, ma'am," Dahlia murmured. She lifted her chin in what Emmy always thought of as Dahlia's stuck-up pose.

But this time she wasn't stuck-up, just determined to keep her voice steady long enough to have her say. "Right after the storm me and Priscilla went out on the Dowdys' big front porch to swing awhile. Tennie was someplace else, but right then she came walking across the yard. She stopped when she saw me." Dahlia paused and looked at her family. Everyone was paying strict attention to her story. "She looked at me real hard. 'What're you doing in my house?' she said. I didn't know what was the matter with her, and neither did Priscilla. 'I'm playing with Priscilla, like I always do,' I said. Then... then she said those awful words." Dahlia hid her face in her hands.

Ma sighed. "Dahlia, just what did Tennie say to you that's got you so upset?"

"Tennie called me 'white trash.' She said our whole family is nothing but white trash."

"Well, coming from Tennie, that shouldn't have shocked you," Ma said.

"She's about as stuck on herself as anybody can get," Emmy added.

"But she had a reason for saying that," Dahlia said. "Tennie saw Gene going into the mines this morning with his lunch pail. She said nobody but white trash sends their kids off to work in the mines when they're just fourteen." Dahlia looked up at Ma. "Is it true? Is Gene working in the mines now?"

Ma looked toward Pa's door and frowned. "Hush, Dahlia," she said. "Your pa will hear you."

"But, Ma, you swore nobody else in the family would go in the mines."

A look of pain crossed Ma's face.

Emmy jumped up from the table. "Stop it, Dahlia," she said. "You don't know anything about it."

"How come I don't know? It's not fair...."

Ma sighed. "You're right. I knew we wouldn't be able to keep it from everybody for long. But I figured the fewer people who knew, the less likely your pa would be to find out." She brushed a strand of hair back from Dahlia's face. "Gene had to go to work in the mines so we could go on living in this house. Now, you go comb your hair and come set the table for me."

Dahlia marched out of the kitchen, her head once more high. But Emmy saw her chin quiver and knew her look of defiance was just for show.

The rain started up again, so baseball practice was called off and only three boarders came for supper.

When Gene got home, his face was so masked by coal dust that Kate and Marvin shied into a corner, not knowing who he was. Ma had a large kettle of water heated on the cookstove and Gene dumped the water into a basin on the back porch and quietly washed up.

The afternoon's activities had tired Pa out so that when Emmy took his supper in to him, she found him sound asleep, his good arm flung over his face.

NEXT MORNING, SATURDAY, the sun was out again.

"As soon as you get done there," Ma said to Emmy, who was washing the breakfast dishes, "you and Everett each take a couple of buckets up to the train line and get us some more coal. Maybe with the rain last night nobody went out to gather it."

Lumps of coal fell off the overloaded trains as they rumbled through the town, and by looking carefully Emmy and Everett could usually find coal along the tracks near their house. But the best place to gather coal was near the tipple, the mine opening where the miners went underground. When full freight cars pulled away from the loading chute, some coal always shook loose and fell alongside the tracks.

Emmy and Everett never went all the way up to the chute when they were picking up coal—they felt that was coal company property, and they didn't want the men who worked the machinery to shout at them and chase them away. Instead, they picked up coal that fell where the train rounded the first bend as it headed away from the tipple.

"Ma was right," Everett said as they neared the bend. "We'll get these buckets full in a hurry today."

Emmy slipped on a pair of blackened gloves. They were a pair Pa used to wear and were so big the fingers doubled under at the ends of her own fingers. Though the gloves made her hands clumsy, Emmy always wore them because they were Pa's.

Everett's bare hands flew among the coal lumps, tossing one after another into a bucket. By the time Emmy had filled her first bucket, he was well under way on his second. Emmy rested for a minute, sitting back on her heels. Overhead, the sun was peeking over the mountains and beginning to pour its heat into the hollow where the mine lay. Soon the day would be hot, too hot to be in the kitchen where the stove fire had to be kept going all day to cook the boarders' meals. But for a few minutes the sun was welcome, laying heat like a blessing along the track and into the ditches, drying last night's puddles and burning away the fog that hung over the mountains.

Emmy sighed with contentment. "This is a lot better than trying to gather coal last winter," she said.

"Yeah, I don't even want to think about that," Everett said.

"Remember how we had to get coal out of the creek?"

Everett nodded. "And it was near impossible to fill even one bucket. But we had to keep the fire burning in the coal grate for the boarders, and the kitchen stove hot enough to heat Pa's room."

In past years, when Pa was working, the Mourfields could afford to buy the coal they needed. But after Pa's accident, Emmy and Everett picked up coal regularly. Other kids were there, too. Families that couldn't afford to buy coal scoured the railroad tracks for enough fuel to keep their houses warm and to cook their food.

The first time she had gone, Emmy was filled with shame. She had stooped to her work, not looking at anyone, scarcely answering the greetings of friends. Everett had called out to everyone, laughing with the others at the blackness of his hands, and had even gotten into a coal-throwing fight with another boy.

In February, when the weather turned bitter, coal was hard to find. On some of those days, Emmy and Everett had to go into the creek below the track to gather lumps that had rolled down the hill, the only lumps left available if other people had gotten to the tracks ahead of them. Sometimes ice formed on the creek, and they would break the thin crust by rolling a large rock into the water. Their shoes always got wet as they waded in, and their hands, despite gloves, became red and so numb they could scarcely feel the coal.

Still, they managed to gather enough to keep the fires going even in the worst weather.

And now, in the summer, Ma was already looking ahead, and for each bucket of coal she burned, she would dump another bucket into a boarded-up corner of the backyard. After all, Gene wasn't near as skilled at mining coal as Pa, and he wouldn't earn as much. They'd still need to pick up coal.

But right now, Emmy refused to think beyond the day and the welcome sunshine.

Ten

"THE WAY THAT SUNSHINE LOOKS, they'll be playing ball today," Everett said as he and Emmy walked back home on the crossties, each carrying two buckets filled with coal. "Me and Jim Bob will be right there, carrying water and setting up the bats. You want to go with me?"

Emmy put her buckets down for a minute to rest her arms. She preferred carrying coal to carrying water—at least coal didn't slosh out all over her shoes or onto her bare feet—but neither load was easy to tote.

"Do you think Ma will let me go if I ask her?" she said.

"Heck, no. And if you ask her, she'll know I'm going."

"But she'd probably let you go to a game here in town," Emmy said.

"Yeah, I reckon she would. Unless she found out I'd already slipped out to that game in Pikesbury."

"So what are you going to do—just go on slipping out to practices and games all summer?"

Everett frowned. "Well, I haven't thought it through yet." Then he smiled. "But today I'm going to go."

Emmy picked up her buckets and tried to match her stride to Everett's easy step from crosstie to crosstie. "Well, I guess I'll just go, too," she said.

Everett grinned at her.

Ma had the meal prepared and simmering on the back of the stove when Emmy and Everett got home. She stoked the fire with several lumps of the coal they had brought in. "I'm aiming to get started canning the first of the tomatoes," she said, pointing to several baskets filled with tomatoes.

Emmy and Dahlia set about boiling jars to sterilize them and washing tomatoes while Everett carried more water. As Emmy worked, she glanced occasionally at her sister. Dahlia's previous storm of emotion about Gene had gone now, just as surely as the rainstorm had passed over. But something else had gone as well. The red bow was missing from Dahlia's hair, and the half-proud, half-defiant lift of her chin was missing, too. She had worked all morning without once mentioning going to Priscilla's.

"All right, girls," Ma said. "Those tomatoes look fine. Now I'll pour scalding water over them, and you can slip their skins off."

She lifted a kettle of boiling water, carried it to the table, and poured it over a washbasin full of tomatoes. As soon as a tomato heated all the way through, Emmy spooned it out of the water, plunged it into a pan of cool water, and passed it to Dahlia, who pierced the skin with a paring knife and slid off the shining red peel. Then Ma pushed the tomato into one of the sterilized half-gallon jars.

Everett placed the full jars into a pot of hot water on the stove. Ma wiped the jar tops and screwed on the lids. The four of them worked easily together. Canning tomatoes had been a summer ritual since Emmy could remember. Even before they had boarders to worry about, they had preserved their own food in the summer.

Kate and Marvin came into the kitchen. Marvin was rubbing his eyes and whining. He went straight to Ma and clung to her leg.

"Kate, see what you can do with him," Ma said. "We don't need young'uns around all this boiling water."

"Come on, Marvin," Kate said, "we'll go play on the back porch."

Marvin shook his head and wrapped his arms more tightly around Ma's leg. "Don't wanna," he wailed.

"Kate..." Ma said, stepping back from the stove, dragging Marvin along with her.

Kate tried to pry Marvin's arms loose from Ma's leg. Marvin cried louder.

"What in tarnation is going on in there?" Pa yelled.

Ma picked Marvin up. "Everything is all right, Frank," she called.

Marvin went on wailing.

"It don't sound to me like things are all right," Pa yelled. "Sounds like somebody is trying to kill one of my young'uns."

Ma stepped to the bedroom door, Marvin in her arms. "He's just sleepy and in a bad mood," she said, smoothing Marvin's hair.

Marvin's cries were muffled as he buried his head against Ma's neck.

"We're trying to can tomatoes, but we can't work with Marvin underfoot," Ma said.

"Well, just send those least ones in here," Pa said. "A body can't rest anyway with all that racket."

Kate smiled and marched into Pa's bedroom. "Will you play the banjo for me today, Pa?" she asked.

The tomato wobbled in Emmy's spoon, fell onto the table, and slid toward Dahlia.

"Emmy, watch out!" Dahlia said sharply as she caught the tomato with the tip of her paring knife.

Emmy ignored her, staring at the door to Pa's room.

Marvin was clamoring now to get out of Ma's arms. "Pa's banjo," he said gleefully.

Finally Pa spoke. "All right, child," he said, "we'll play the banjo."

"Frank…, " Ma said. She took a step into the room, behind Marvin.

"It's all right, Sally," Pa said in almost a growl. "Just find my banjo and hand it here."

Ma disappeared into the room. Emmy slowly let out her breath and looked at Everett. He, too, had stopped what he was doing to stare at the door. Only Dahlia went on with her work.

"I'm out of tomatoes, Emmy," Dahlia said. Then she looked from Emmy to Everett. "What's the matter with you two?" Her glance followed theirs to the bedroom door. "Oh," she said quietly.

They had all missed Pa's music since his accident. How was Pa, with only one arm, going to play the banjo?

"Here it is, Frank." Ma's voice was muffled because she was pulling the banjo out from the back of the wardrobe.

Kate clapped and laughed. Marvin's laugh rang out in unison.

Ma came back into the kitchen. Everett, Emmy, and Dahlia were still staring at the doorway.

"We're never going to get those tomatoes canned," Ma said. She took up another sterilized jar and began pushing tomatoes into it.

With Everett's help, Emmy set the washbasin on the stove to reheat the water that had cooled too much to loosen the tomato skins.

All four of them tried to concentrate on canning tomatoes, but when the first tentative musical note came from the bedroom, the work stopped again. The note was repeated several times, its pitch changing with each repeat.

"That's it," Pa said. "We've got the **B** string tuned."

The corners of Ma's mouth turned up slightly. She stepped briskly to the stove and put the lid on the kettle of filled tomato jars. Then she surveyed the dwindled pile of tomatoes. "Let's get these few ready to can as soon as the first ones have boiled thirty minutes."

Emmy sometimes thought Ma was happiest when she was canning, or maybe that was when she was almost her happiest. Her best moments seemed to be when she was out in her garden. Planting, hoeing, or picking—it didn't seem to matter to Ma as long as she was working around the soil. Pa's accident had taken the edge off the enjoyment even of her gardening and canning, but now she looked almost like her old self.

However, the sounds coming from the bedroom weren't like Pa's old music. There were no recognizable melodies, just the sound of one string being tested against another with long pauses in between, during which time Emmy tried to imagine Pa handling the banjo with his good hand and the stump of his other arm.

Kate and Marvin didn't seem to mind the lack of songs. Each time Pa pronounced a string tuned, they clapped and squealed.

By the time the first jars of tomatoes came out of their water bath, Pa had tuned the fifth string. Emmy waited for the real music to begin, but the bedroom was quiet.

Then Kate came into the kitchen, pulling Marvin along behind her. Marvin was whining and digging in his heels. "Pa won't play a song for us," Kate said, sounding ready to cry.

"Dahlia, we're caught up enough in here," Ma said. "You take the little ones out back and see if you can get them settled down." She turned to Emmy. "Take some water and a washrag in to your pa. Everett, you and me can get these last jars set into the water bath. Then I reckon you better go see if there's enough berries left to make picking this evening worthwhile."

"Yes, ma'am," each said in turn.

Emmy dipped some of the hot water from the reservoir in the stove and poured it into a small washbasin. She took down a towel and washrag from the line behind the stove. When she walked into Pa's room, he was lying with his back toward the door. The banjo lay at the foot of the bed.

She set the washbasin on the stand beside the bed. "Ma thought you might like to wash up a little, Pa," she said.

Pa didn't move, so Emmy wet the cloth and wiped off the back of his neck. He was soaked with perspiration. As she ran the washcloth over his left cheek and around his closed eye, she wasn't sure all the dampness on his face was from perspiration. She patted dry the part of his face she could reach and the back of his neck.

"Just leave me be. I'm fine," Pa said without turning over.

Emmy picked up the banjo. "I'll put your banjo beside the bed."

"Put it back in the wardrobe," Pa said.

"But you've got it all tuned...."

Pa rolled over to face her. "I told you to put it back where it belongs." He clamped his mouth in a straight line, and his eyes looked cold and hard.

"Yes, Pa," Emmy said quietly.

She picked up the banjo carefully, not touching any of the strings, and laid it on a blanket in the bottom of the wardrobe. She wasn't sure how long a banjo would stay in tune if no one played it. Pa had worked hard to tune it. She wondered again how he would play it with only one hand. Even more, she wondered if he would ever want to try.

Eleven

MA AND EMMY WERE SETTING the last jars of tomatoes on the table to cool when Everett came whistling into the kitchen. "Looka here," he said, extending his cap. "The last of the berries. I picked enough to put in a little bowl with some sugar and milk so's Marvin can have a treat. But there's not enough for us to go up there with buckets."

Ma sighed. "Well, everything comes to an end sooner or later. But it sure was nice to have all those free berries to make into pies. I guess I'll have to start making butterscotch or vinegar pies."

Emmy licked her lips. One of her favorite desserts was butterscotch pie, a creamy mix of brown sugar, milk, butter, and eggs, all topped with a meringue of stiffly beaten egg whites and sugar, browned in the oven so the peaks of meringue were toasty curlicues. She liked vinegar pie, too, though the name of it was enough to pucker her lips. But the dab of vinegar left no taste by the time Ma stirred together sugar, eggs, and a little flour. Emmy liked blackberry pie also, but she was about tired of it. She was even more tired of picking blackberries.

Now, with no blackberries to pick, there was nothing in the way of her going to the game with Everett. Nothing, that is, except Ma.

Gene was working only half a shift this Saturday, and he came in while everyone, except Pa, was gathered around the table. The door to Pa's bedroom was shut, as it had been the last few hours.

Gene grinned at Ma, his teeth a white flash against his coal-blackened face. "I've sent word to the Slones about the lumber for your chicken house. If we hear back from them that they've got slabs they won't be needing, Everett and Emmy and me can borrow a wagon and go over and get them."

"And me," Dahlia said. "I want to go, too."

"Well, shoot, yes," Gene said, reaching out a grimy hand to tousle her hair. "We'll take any able hands that can load a plank or two."

Dahlia ducked in time to avoid coal-dust-streaked hair, but she grinned at Gene. Emmy noticed Dahlia was not so standoffish around Gene. Maybe it was a case of the loners teaming together.

Everett washed the dishes while Emmy dried. Dahlia was on the back porch, washing Kate and Marvin's feet, getting them ready for a nap. Gene was bathing in the backyard, and Ma had gone into Pa's room to try to talk him into eating some dinner.

"We just got time to get down to the ballpark before they throw out the first ball," Everett said, glancing at the kitchen clock.

"What're we going to tell Ma?" Emmy asked.

"Let's go while she's in Pa's room. We'll let Dahlia tell her we're gone."

They hurriedly put the dishes on the shelf and hung the towels to dry behind the stove. Emmy kept one eye on the bedroom door. She didn't think she could fool Ma, and she wasn't sure she had enough nerve to try.

Dahlia was drying Marvin's feet as Everett and Emmy went out the back door.

"Tell Ma Emmy and me will be with Jim Bob for a while," Everett said over his shoulder.

"Did Ma say you could go?" Dahlia asked.

"Ma's busy, so we didn't ask her," Everett said breezily.

"She's not going to like it," Dahlia warned.

Emmy didn't dare look at her sister. She was sure Dahlia would guess she and Everett were up to more than just a visit with Jim Bob.

"Come on," Everett urged as they waved to Gene, who was dressed in clean clothes and dumping his bathwater over Ma's flowers.

Jim Bob was waiting on the road in front of his house. "Well, well," he said when he saw Emmy. "Are we heading down to the creek to cool off?"

Everett looked puzzled. "Heck, no, Jim Bob. You know we're going to the ball game."

Emmy felt like stomping Jim Bob's bare toes. But right now she wanted to go to the ball game more than she wanted to shut him up, so she just smiled as he fell in step with her and Everett.

Before they reached the baseball diamond—laid on a flat piece of land near the creek—they heard people calling to one another and the occasional crack of a ball hit by a bat.

"Come on," Everett said, breaking into a run. "They're gonna start before we get there."

Emmy and Jim Bob followed him. By the time they got to the diamond, the home team had taken the field. The men passed the ball around the bases, each smacking his fist into his glove while he waited for the ball to be thrown to him. The first batter was loosening up near home plate. He held the bat behind his back and stretched from side to side.

"Play ball," the umpire yelled.

The batter raised the bat over his head, reached it as far in front of his body as his arms would stretch, straightened, and walked to the plate.

"Strike him out," someone called.

"Knock it to kingdom come," one of the visitors shouted.

"Let's find Petey," Jim Bob said.

Emmy followed Everett and Jim Bob. They found Petey squatted near the end of the home-team bench, a weed stuck between his teeth.

"Me and Everett are here," Jim Bob said.

Petey waved to him, but he didn't take his eyes off the ball as it sped from the pitcher's hand across the plate.

"Stri-i-i-ke one!" the umpire called.

On the field the players popped their fists in their gloves and shouted encouragingly to the pitcher. The visitors, on a bench across from where Emmy, Everett, and Jim Bob stood, shuffled their feet and called encouragingly to the batter. The pitcher wound up and threw the baseball again.

"Stri-i-i-ke two!"

"You 'bout got him now," a fan called.

"Ball one!" the umpire shouted after the next pitch.

"Get some glasses, ump," called one of the men standing near the home-team bench.

Emmy sat down on the bench. She watched the game almost as intently as Petey did, but her attention went from the pitcher to the batter and around the field to each player. She had forgotten how much she liked to attend baseball games, how she used to enjoy the sight of these ordinarily hardworking men laughing and squabbling and playing as if they were Jim Bob and Everett's age. When they shed their miners' hats and put on their baseball caps, they shed their years, too. She wished Pa were beside her. He still had his eyes and his ears, and he probably could still shout and joke. But was he ever going to come out of the bedroom so he could see and hear that the world was still like it had always been?

The pitcher struck the first batter out, but he wasn't as lucky with the next batter. His second pitch, a fast ball just below the batter's waist, was what the batter was looking for. He swung hard. The crack of the bat meeting the ball silenced the Baileytown fans. The ball sailed over the heads of the fielders, beyond the creek winding around the diamond, and into a clump of trees. The batter loped around the bases, waving his hat to his teammates when he crossed home plate.

"Heck," Jim Bob said, slapping his hand on the bench.

The next batter hit a grounder, scooped up by the second baseman. The batter was out at first. Petey stood up after the fourth batter was called out on strikes. "They'll be needing some water," he said to Everett and Jim Bob.

Emmy slid off the bench with the two boys. Even though they didn't need her help, she didn't want to sit on the bench alone. She was the only girl around, and she wondered why she hadn't thought to wear a pair of Everett's britches and to stuff her hair into an old cap. Then she laughed. What would Dahlia have told Ma if she'd seen Emmy going out of the house dressed like a boy?

The men drank, sloshed a little water on their faces, and sat on the bench, each waiting his turn at bat. Everett and Jim Bob picked up the empty buckets and hurried to the water pump half a mile back down the road.

"You don't have to come with us," Everett said as Emmy followed them. "You can stay and watch our team bat. Me and Jim Bob always miss the first few batters."

Jim Bob nodded. "But it's better than missing *all* the batters when the game's away from home, like we used to do before we got to be official water boys."

There was a certain ring to Jim Bob's voice when he said *water boys*, sort of the way he might say *president of the United States*. Emmy didn't see that it was much fun to carry water—heaven knew both boys did enough of that at home—but she had to admit it would be fun to be able to go to all the games. She never envied Everett when he was hauling out ashes or doing some heavy lifting for Ma, but maybe there were some advantages to being a boy.

"I'd rather come with you," she said.

The water pump sat on the square near the clubhouse and soda fountain. The area was quiet. On weekdays, while the miners were underground, the accountants and other office workers sometimes walked around the square or sat on benches beneath the silver maples. And on Saturday and Sunday afternoons, except when a home baseball game drew everybody out to the diamond, the square was filled with people—with miners who couldn't seem to get enough sun during the few hours they were above ground and with children who ran through the grass and swung on the pipe railings that outlined the square.

"Come on," Jim Bob said when the water buckets were full. Each boy carried two, and water sloshed over their bare feet as the three of them hurried back to the ball field.

Before they reached the ball field, Emmy saw two girls walking toward them. Even from a distance she could see they wore shoes and starched and ironed dresses. Then she recognized Tennie and Priscilla.

Tennie looped her arm through Priscilla's and moved her to the far side of the road. "On Saturday afternoons the white trash runs around looking like ragamuffins," Tennie said.

Priscilla looked quickly at Emmy, flushed, and hurried past.

"La-dee-dah," Jim Bob said, tilting his chin as high as he could. "Looks like Miss Hootie-Tootie's sister is getting just like her. All this mining town needs is another girl stuck on herself."

Emmy knew the girls heard Jim Bob, but they didn't reply. She watched them go down the road, arm in arm.

Twelve

DAHLIA WAS IN THE BACKYARD when Emmy and Everett got home. She was playing "house" by herself, arranging rocks for furniture and sticks for people. Emmy thought of Priscilla and Tennie's haughtiness, and she felt a twinge of sadness at seeing her sister so completely alone. But the twinge vanished when Dahlia looked up with a smirk.

"Ma wants to see you, Emmy," she said. "I told her what you said, and she didn't like it one little bit. I bet you're going to get a licking."

Emmy didn't believe Dahlia's threat of a licking for one minute. Ma had never whipped any of them. Back when he was healthy, Pa had sometimes taken a belt to Everett and Gene, but even he didn't believe in lickings for girls. Emmy had always been afraid of getting a licking at school, where the teachers punished anyone who got out of line, both boys and girls.

Ma was in the kitchen rolling out pastry for pies. "There you are," she said, brushing back a strand of hair and leaving a streak of flour across her forehead. "Dahlia told me you'd gone off with Everett and Jim Bob."

"Yes, ma'am."

"You certainly were gone a long time."

"Yes, ma'am." Emmy kept her eyes downcast, knowing if she looked up, Ma would see the guilt in her face.

Everett came to her rescue. "Ma, you oughta see what me and Jim Bob have made. It's the best turtle trap in the world."

"And what're you aiming to do with a turtle trap?" Ma asked, turning her attention away from Emmy.

"Well, we've got it set up down at the creek...."

While Everett explained the turtle trap, Emmy filled a glass with water and slipped into Pa's room. He was lying back against the pillows, his eyes closed, his breathing steady. Emmy wished she could tell him about the ball game, about the final out with the bases loaded, the high pop-fly going past the pitcher and the shortstop, going on over the head of the center fielder so that all those watching held their breaths. Then the right fielder running in from nowhere, getting under the ball, and finally the smack of the ball in his glove. And the game was over, the home team losing by one run with all those men left on base.

Pa would have liked being there, even if they did lose.

ON MONDAY, after the boarders' supper, Ma, Dahlia, and Emmy dished up plates of food for Kate and Marvin, who sat at the kitchen table. Gene was still at work, and Everett had slipped out.

"Everett sure is spending a lot of time lately running around with Jim Bob," Ma said. "They must be determined to catch that turtle."

Dahlia looked at Emmy, who made her face a blank mask. She went on spooning up small new potatoes cooked in their red skins, chives from Ma's garden snipped over the top of them.

Suddenly they heard a noise in Pa's room—the thud of a chair being picked up and set down hard. The thudding noise came again, and again ten seconds or so later, this time closer.

After another minute, Pa appeared in the doorway, leaning on the back of the chair that usually sat by his bed.

"Frank…" Ma began, taking a step toward him.

Pa shook his head vigorously. "I'm all right, woman," he said. "I aimed to see if any of the other four walls look as bad as the ones in my room." He looked around. Then he smiled. "I reckon they do."

Kate jumped up. "Come eat supper with us, Pa," she yelled.

Pa leaned his shoulder against the doorway, his right hand still holding the chair. He seemed to be counting the steps that separated him from the table. Then he sighed. "Some other time, Kate," he said. "I reckon I've done used up my strength."

"Let me help you, Frank," Ma said.

Again Pa stopped her with a shake of his head. "I made it here. I'll make it back." He turned, pulling the chair around with him.

They all waited quietly, listening to the chair thudding across the bedroom.

Ma smiled frequently during supper. Emmy, too, felt relieved that Pa had finally gotten out of bed. Maybe now he was going to try to get his strength back, to come to the table and eat with them. Maybe he would even sit on the porch and speak to the people who passed on the road. Maybe one day he would go down to the soda fountain….

When Emmy took some food in to him later, Pa was asleep. He woke before she could leave the room. "Come on over here," he said.

She set the food on the nightstand, but Pa waved it away and patted the bed. "Sit down awhile, girl," he said.

Emmy sat. She could sense Pa's rare good mood, and she fished around in her mind for something to tell him that wouldn't destroy it. Mining talk would upset him. Most of the boarders' talk was against the unions, and Emmy knew that would upset Pa. Finally she said, "Could we sing a song, Pa?"

Pa nodded.

Emmy looked closely at him. He was still relaxed. She decided to try one more thing, even at the risk of sending him back into his black mood.

"Do you think your banjo is still in tune, Pa?"

Pa narrowed his eyes. "I don't reckon it'd be in perfect tune, but it oughta be a lot closer than it was last week."

"If I got it for you, would you play something?"

"All I got left is my strumming hand. A body can't make music lessen he can chord."

"But, Pa…"

"You heard me." He clamped his lips shut. Emmy felt annoyed with herself. Now she had done it.

Then Pa's expression softened. "Lessen, of course, you'd like to play it yourself."

"Me?"

"Sure. You got my blood in you, and I reckon my blood's got enough music in it to stretch over another generation."

Emmy stared at him. Back when Pa played his banjo all the time, he always put it on top of the wardrobe when he got through, well out of reach of any little ones in the house. Even Gene never tried playing Pa's banjo.

She went to the wardrobe and got the banjo. She carried it to Pa's bed and sat down next to him.

"Just take the neck of it in your left hand," said Pa. "Rest it on your palm and curl your fingers over the strings."

The banjo felt smooth, the wood well worn from years of Pa's handling. Now Emmy's hands held the banjo. Despite Pa's assurance that she had music in her blood, she didn't feel at all confident.

"Strum it a little to get the feel," Pa said.

Emmy drew the fingers of her right hand quickly across the strings, the way she'd seen Pa do so many times. There was no music, just an awkward-sounding thunk. The strings were surprisingly tough, not soft and yielding the way they looked when Pa strummed them.

Pa laughed. "Well, I don't reckon you'd wake the dead if that's all the music you can get out of it. Try again."

This time Emmy pressed her fingers against the strings and drew her hand deliberately across them. Each string plunked beneath her fingers, but the sound was anything but musical.

"Do it again," Pa said.

She did.

"Again."

She drew her fingers over the strings again and again until gradually the sounds from the separate strings began to blend together. But it was still a discordant sound, and her fingers were getting so sore she expected to see blood dripping from them—the blood Pa thought had some music in it.

Finally Pa nodded. "I reckon with enough practice you might get a song out of that banjo. But you got to learn some chords."

"Can you show me where to put my fingers?" Emmy asked, handing the banjo to Pa.

Pa took the banjo hesitantly. "I don't know as I can figure it with the wrong hand." He laid the banjo across his lap, cradling the neck of it in his right hand. He pressed his little finger on a string. "You'll have to reach over and strum for me," he said.

Emmy moved closer. She strummed the strings awkwardly. Still, a sound close to music came from the instrument. Pa nodded and moved his fingers into another position. Once more Emmy strummed.

"Hey, that don't sound like a cat with its tail under a rocker no more," Gene said from the doorway.

"Come on in," said Pa, laying the banjo aside. "You been making yourself scarce since you got back from Slones'. Where you been keeping yourself?"

"Just here and there," Gene answered.

"I reckon more there than here."

"I've found plenty to keep me busy," Gene replied.

Emmy looked from one to the other. They were a lot alike, Pa and Gene—the high cheekbones, the jutting chin that created a horizontal line below the lower lip. And they were alike in other ways—they both had the same determination that caused their chins to jut out.

"Come over here closer to the bed so's I can see you better," Pa said.

Gene took a few more steps toward Pa.

"I said come on over here." Pa's voice rose.

Emmy slid off the bed as Gene crossed the floor.

Pa peered at Gene. "Open the curtain," he said, nodding to Emmy.

As Emmy pulled open the curtain, the room's dimness vanished and the waning daylight streamed in, spreading across Pa's bed and over Gene. Pa blinked in the light, but Gene stood unmoving.

"Let me see your hands," said Pa

Gene held out his hands. Pa took one and examined the palm.

"Reckon you've still got the calluses of a lumber man," Pa said.

"Yes, sir. I ain't gone soft yet."

Then Pa turned Gene's hand over and peered at the fingernails. "Reckon you've got a lot of coal dust on your fingers." He gripped Gene's hand tightly. "It wouldn't be that your ma has got you picking up coal for the stoves, would it?"

"No, sir," Gene said, unflinching under what Emmy knew was a very strong grasp.

"You been putting in folks' gardens in this black soil?"

"No, sir."

"You been scrubbing stoves and chimneys?"

"No, sir."

"Then how in tarnation did you get such stained fingers?"

Gene swallowed hard. "Pa, I ain't going to lie to you," he said in a soft voice.

Pa dropped Gene's hand suddenly and grabbed his shirt, pulling Gene's face down close to his. "Even from across the room I could see your eyes, and I knew it. You're getting raccoon eyes."

Emmy looked at Gene. She hadn't noticed before. But then she usually only saw Gene very early in the morning or late in the evening. Pa was right—it would have been obvious to anyone looking carefully. Gene had been in the mines for only a few weeks, and already he was getting what the miners called "raccoon eyes," the area around the eyes so embedded with coal dust that it could not be scrubbed completely clean

Pa turned Gene loose and fell back on the pillows. "Good God, son. What are we doing to you?"

"Pa, it's all right—" Gene began.

But Pa sat upright again. "The devil it's all right. Sally!" he shouted. He grabbed the bell from beside his bed and began shaking it.

Thirteen

MA RUSHED INTO THE ROOM. "Frank, what is it? Are you…?" She stopped when she saw Gene standing in the fading sunlight beside Pa's bed.

Pa dropped the bell. "I want to know what's going on in this family. Who in tarnation decided Gene was going to go down in the mines?" Pa was no longer shouting, his voice now cold and hard.

Ma straightened her back. "I decided that, Frank."

"You decided that! You…Who told you to make that decision?"

"No one had to tell me, Frank. It was the only way to stay here."

"To stay here? You mean the company…?"

"You know the rules—the houses are for company people. If you don't have someone working for the company, you don't live in one of the houses." Ma shrugged. "They thought they had been kind to let us…."

A red flush crept up Pa's neck and over his face. "Kind!" he shouted. "They name it a kindness to near kill a man in their mines, to make him useless as a bucket full of holes?"

Ma reached a hand toward Pa. "Frank, there isn't any need to get all wrought up."

For a second Emmy feared that Pa was going to strike down Ma's hand, but instead he jerked his head out of her reach. "Well, I ain't gonna stand for it," he said, his voice becoming calm again. "I ain't gonna let them take my son and do the same thing to him."

"Pa, I don't mind loading coal," Gene said. "The other men have warned me about fire damp, and how the gases can explode; and black damp, when the oxygen gives out; and—"

"Yes, and I reckon someday you'll find out firsthand about roof timbers falling in. Or maybe, worse yet, you'll learn all about *white* damp, the smell like violets down in the dark mines, the gas coming after an explosion somewhere in the mines or even sometimes creeping in after somebody has been blasting. The smell not many men live to tell about." Pa looked at Gene intently. "I reckon that's the next lesson you'll learn down in the mines."

"Now, Pa...."

Ma silenced Gene with a wave of her hand. "There's no need to argue about this. I don't want Gene down in the mines either. Do you think I like living every day knowing what the mines did to you, Frank, and knowing one of my sons is down there now and that something might happen to him any minute? And that he might not even be lucky enough to come out alive?"

"Alive!" Pa snorted. "Sometimes it ain't lucky to be left alive."

Ma ignored him. "I hate the mines. I always have, and I always will." She gazed straight ahead. "My family didn't want the life of a coal miner's wife for me. My Pa said coal companies were ruining the land, and he wouldn't have any of his family in the coal towns. I chose you, Frank, even though it meant going against my own kin. I would do it again," she said, her voice softening. "A body does what she has to do. We got little ones that have to be fed and given a half-decent place to live. I'll do what has to be done to see they're taken care of."

Ma laid a hand briefly on Gene's shoulder. Then she turned and went back to the kitchen.

"Pa," Gene said.

Pa looked up. "Get out," he said. "There ain't nothing I can do to help nobody." He jerked his legs violently, sending the banjo crashing to the floor. The sound of cracking wood echoed through the room.

"Oh, Pa!" Emmy cried.

"It don't matter," Pa said. "Take it out and get rid of it. I got no more need for it."

Emmy picked up the broken banjo, cradling it in her arms.

FOR THE NEXT FEW DAYS Pa didn't ring his bell at all. The family took food and water in to him, washed his body when he became hot and sweaty, and left clean shirts for him to put on, but he lay listlessly, staring beyond whoever tried to help him.

One evening Nick Hall came by. When Emmy told Pa Nick was there, Pa's expression remained as vacant as it had been all week. But he didn't say to send Nick away, so Emmy told Nick to go on in. She left him sitting in the chair, recounting some story from the mines, laughing and laying a hand on Pa's shoulder.

Later Nick joined the family sitting on the front porch. "He's sunk about low as I've ever seen him," he said to Ma.

Ma nodded, but she didn't say anything.

"I come by hoping he'd go to a meeting with me tomorrow evening. But he wouldn't hear of it," Nick said. Then he faced Gene, who sat on the porch railing. "Reckon you'll be there?"

"I don't know," Gene said. "I've heard the men talking, but if Pa don't approve...."

"Well, every man has to decide for his family, but I'm aiming to be there." Nick said good-bye and walked down the steps.

Ma turned to Gene. "Union activities?" she asked.

"Yes. An organizer's been working this part of the mountains most of the summer. That's about all the men talk about when no coal-company officials are around."

"What does the coal company say about him?"

"Well, mostly they don't say anything. Right now they got more coal they need dug than they got miners. But the word is if things get tight again, it'll be the men siding with the union that'll get laid off first."

"Are you aiming to join them?" Ma asked.

"I ain't studying on it right now. All I got time for is learning to be a miner."

"I don't know what we'd do without you, son," Ma said quietly.

The week seemed very long to Emmy. Pa's despair had settled on all the family, and even their meals were silent. On Saturday Everett got ready to go to another baseball game. Even though Ma had forgotten about Emmy's being away last weekend, and no more questions had been asked, this game was in another coal town, and Emmy didn't dare chance going.

She sat on the porch and watched Everett go off to meet Jim Bob. The afternoon stretched ahead of her—several hours without any demands on her time. The kitchen was clean. Kate and Marvin were taking a nap. Dahlia, who hadn't seen Priscilla since that awful day, was playing at another friend's house. Pa was in his room, and Ma, who never seemed to stop, was lying on the sofa in the sitting room, the curtains closed and a damp cloth on her forehead.

Emmy thought about going down to the creek to check the turtle trap, but the prospect of coming face-to-face with a trapped snapping turtle didn't appeal to her. Then she thought about Pa's banjo.

When he had told her to get rid of it, she had hidden it away in her corner of the bedroom. Because she, Dahlia, Kate, and Marvin shared the front bedroom, they each had made a private place where they could put personal belongings without anyone bothering them. Kate and Marvin each had an old wooden box tucked under Marvin's cot. Dahlia kept her secret treasures in one corner of the bedroom, and Emmy kept hers in another. The corners were curtained off with old sheets hung on strings, making triangular closets. Their everyday clothing hung on nails in the closets—good clothes hung in the wardrobe in Pa's bedroom.

Emmy had propped the banjo in her corner, behind a feed sack that held her prized possessions—the only book she owned, a copy of Grimm's *Fairy Tales* that had belonged to Ma; a rag doll her grandma had made for her years ago; three rocks tumbled smooth by the creek waters; and a feather from Mrs. Bradford's old rooster. Pa had sharpened the feather shaft into a point, and Emmy used to write with it, dipping it into ink she made by squashing pokeberries into a reddish purple liquid.

She crept into the bedroom and pulled the banjo out from her corner. Tiptoeing, she carried it outdoors and around to the backyard.

Recalling what Pa had taught her wasn't easy, but she remembered the smooth feel of the wood and the firm resistance of the strings beneath her fingers. Despite the crack in the back of the banjo, the wood was still comforting to her hands.

She pressed the little finger of her left hand against the first D string. Because Pa had used his right hand for chording, she had to try to recall all he had done and then reverse the order of fingers. When she was satisfied with her fingering, she strummed the strings. The noise wasn't exactly music, but she figured the problem was the banjo player and not the banjo itself. The crack in the wood affected the mellowness of the notes, but it didn't make the banjo unusable. She was glad she hadn't obeyed Pa and gotten rid of it.

After strumming for a few minutes, she turned the banjo over and examined the crack. It was about two inches long and ran from the center of the back almost to the lower end of the banjo. Not a very big crack, she thought, but enough to make Pa think the banjo had to be thrown away.

But banjos could be fixed. A new back would make the instrument as good as ever. If only she had money to get it repaired for Pa.

Fourteen

On Tuesday evening Gene told the family he'd had word from the Slones. "They said to come on and get all the scrap lumber we can haul. Now," he added, "if we just had some way to haul it."

"I know a way," Everett said. "I bet we can borrow Petey's wagon and mule team."

"You reckon he'd let us?" Gene said.

"Why, sure," Everett said. "He told Jim Bob and me anything he could do to help us out...."

"What makes Petey beholden to you and Jim Bob?" Ma asked.

Everett flushed. Emmy wondered how he was going to get out of this spot. He always seemed to find a way. But Ma was waiting.

"Well, uh, he...," Everett stammered.

Emmy came to his rescue. "Jim Bob's always doing things to help Petey out. And you know how everybody thinks of Jim Bob and Everett as being almost one person." The reasoning sounded lame even to her.

Everett grinned. "Yeah, that's it."

Ma still looked doubtful, but she went back to mending one of Marvin's shirts while Gene and Everett planned the best time to go to the Slones'. Later, when he went off to bed, Everett cuffed Emmy softly on the shoulder, as close as anyone in the family ever came to saying "thank you."

On Thursday Gene's shift at the mine was over early, and he, Everett, Emmy, and Dahlia walked out to the edge of town where Petey kept his team and wagon. They carried a sack packed with cold chicken and chunks of cornbread spread with butter for their supper.

Gene and Everett were having a contest to see who could throw small rocks the greatest distance. Though Gene's muscles were developed from months of logging and weeks of digging coal, his throw was no match for Everett's. Everett selected each stone, weighing it carefully in his hand. He'd wind up like the pitchers did and hurl the stone, leaning into his throw and following through as if his fingers were going to fly through the air after the stone. Gene whooped each time Everett out-threw him.

Dahlia skipped along grinning, giving no thought to the dust coating her legs and dress, unaware that perspiration was causing her hair to stick to her forehead.

Petey had the mules hitched to the wagon, waiting for the Mourfields. "Gosh, you didn't need to go to so much trouble," Gene said.

"No trouble," Petey said. "I'd rather be hitching mules than doing some of the work the old woman thinks up for me." He laughed good-naturedly.

They climbed onto the wagon. Gene sat up front and took the reins loosely in his hand.

As they rode off, Petey called to them. "Don't worry if you're after dark coming back. This team knows its way home from any mining town in these mountains. Doesn't it, Everett?"

"It sure does," Everett called back.

Dahlia looked at Everett as if she were going to ask how he knew about the team. But even she seemed to think an argument would be too much trouble on such a nice day, so she sighed and lay back in the wagon. "I'm going to pretend I'm a princess being taken off to a castle to meet my prince."

Emmy, too, felt a deep sense of peace, so much so that she didn't retort that she shared Dahlia's wish. She often hoped someone would carry Dahlia off—to a castle or to any place out of her own hair.

Two of the Slones, Albert and Willard, were running the sawmill when the Mourfields arrived. "Hey, Gene," Willard called. "Glad you've come back. Pa is about to work us to death."

Gene laughed as he climbed down from the wagon. "I'm not back to work," he said. "Anyway, if you think running that sawmill is hard work, you ought to go down in the mines."

"We heard you're digging coal now," Albert said.

Gene nodded. "But I reckon it's not so bad," he said. "Leastways, I'm not getting sunburned."

The brothers laughed. They pointed to a pile of lumber scraps. "Pa said you were welcome to all you can haul out of here," Willard said. "We'd help you load, but Pa'll skin us alive if we don't have these trees sawed up by the time he drags today's cutting in."

"I brought my own helpers," Gene said.

Everett, Emmy, and Dahlia climbed down from the wagon. Gene led the mules to the stack of scraps, a stack half as tall as a house now that it was summer and no one needed the wood for fires. "Let's put the longest pieces on the bottom," he said. "Everett, you and Emmy be a team, and me and Dahlia'll team up."

They all picked out the longest boards in the stack, lifted them carefully, and laid them the length of the wagon. The smell of fresh lumber filled the air, a smell Emmy thought was as pleasant and promising as springtime in the mountains.

With two people handling each board, the work was easy, even though they sometimes had to move a lot of boards to get to the longest ones.

By the time Mr. Slone drove into the lumberyard, they had almost filled the wagon. Mr. Slone pulled his team up beside the mill, and his sons unhitched the mules. Then he walked over to Gene. "Good to see you again," he said.

"Thank you, sir," Gene said. "These here are my brother and sisters."

Mr. Slone nodded to the three of them. "Looks like you're right good at stacking lumber," he said, walking around the wagon. "That load ought to ride right well."

"We sure are beholden to you for letting us take the planks," Gene said.

Mr. Slone dismissed Gene's thanks with a wave of his hand. "What're you aiming to build with them?" he asked.

"Ma's got it in her head she'd like a chicken house," Gene said.

"Women and their chickens! My Hattie won't eat an egg she hasn't gathered with her own hands." Mr. Slone laughed. "'Course, the boys and me don't fuss none when she fries us up a big skillet of them fresh eggs." He looked over the load of lumber once more. "But building a chicken house takes more than planks. You got everything you need?"

"I'm aiming to go up on the mountainside and cut some cedar poles for the corner posts and some poplar for the beams. I got enough extra planks here to cover the top. I reckon chickens don't mind none if a little rain leaks through."

"Sounds like you got it studied out. Come on down to the shed and we'll get you a bucket of nails," Mr. Slone said.

Everett, Emmy, and Dahlia followed the two past the sawmill and down a hillside. Inside, the shed was dark in the fading daylight, but Mr. Slone lit an oil lamp.

Emmy looked around. The shed was a supply room and an office all in one. In the middle of the room sat a potbelly stove with a few chairs around it, as if the habit of pulling up to the fire was so strong it lasted all year.

Along one wall was a desk—a sturdy piece of furniture with drawers along both sides and topped with shelves and cubbyholes. Papers were stacked on the desk and in every hole. Another wall was lined with deep shelves. Mr. Slone led Gene to that part of the room.

A side wall interested Emmy. On it hung two fiddles, a dulcimer, and a banjo. She walked over to the instruments. They were made of wood, and although she didn't know one kind of wood from another, she recognized beauty in the grains. The wood glowed softly in the lamplight, evidence of hours of smoothing and polishing. She thought about Pa's banjo and the care he used to give it.

"Pa would like to see those, wouldn't he?" Dahlia said at her elbow.

"Once upon a time he would have," Emmy said. "But I don't know now...." She reached up and ran a finger along the side of the banjo. It felt as smooth as it looked.

"Take it down and play it if you've a mind to," Mr. Slone called from across the room.

Emmy drew back her hand. "Oh, no, I don't know how to play. I was just admiring how pretty it is."

Mr. Slone handed Gene a sack partly filled with nails. Then he took down the banjo and handed it to Emmy. "See how good those strings strum," he said.

Feeling shy, Emmy strummed the banjo, the way Pa had taught her. The sound was discordant, but even with her limited musical knowledge, she could tell the banjo had a good tone. "It sure is nice," she said as she gave it back to Mr. Slone.

"Pa used to play the banjo a lot," Dahlia said.

Mr. Slone nodded. "I remember hearing your pa play. He sure could get music out of a banjo. Now me, all I can do is make them and play a little tune or two." Mr. Slone ran a hand along the neck of the banjo. "Your pa…." He hesitated. "Can your pa still play?"

"No," Dahlia said. "He tried one day, but…."

"Anyway, his banjo is broken now," Emmy said quickly. What would Ma say if she knew they were telling their troubles to Mr. Slone?

"What do you mean the banjo is broken?" asked Mr. Slone.

"The back of it. It…it fell off Pa's bed, and the back of it cracked," Emmy said.

"Well, now, that's not so hard to fix. I tell you what, if one of you will fetch that banjo to me, I'll fix it up good as new."

"We couldn't let you do that, Mr. Slone," Gene said. "Our family is already beholden to you for the planks and now for these nails. We thank you kindly, but we can't let you do any more."

Emmy wanted to protest. She knew they shouldn't depend on anyone else, but Mr. Slone's offer didn't sound like charity to her. Gene's mouth was set in that way he and Pa had.

"I don't reckon your family would have to be beholden to me for fixing an old banjo. Anyway, I'd be doing it for these young girls." Mr. Slone motioned to Emmy and Dahlia. "When I see some promising saplings out on the mountainside, I cut away all the scrub trees and let those saplings have light and soil to keep them growing straight and true. I reckon music is sort of like light and soil for people." He looked hard at Gene. "Your pa's music especially."

But Gene shook his head again. "I know you mean it as a kindness, and we thank you for the offer. Pa isn't planning to play that banjo any more." He looked hard at Emmy, as if to say the subject was closed.

On the ride home, Gene gave the mules their head, and he sat on top of the load of lumber with Everett, Emmy, and Dahlia. They ate the chicken and cornbread. Emmy thought it was one of the best suppers she had ever had, and sitting on the good-smelling boards with her sister and brothers was one of the best places she'd ever found to eat supper. She was content to satisfy her hunger while the world grew dark around them—content except for the thought that there ought to be some way she could get Gene to let Mr. Slone fix Pa's banjo.

Fifteen

BUILDING THE CHICKEN HOUSE FILLED their evenings for the next week. Everett let Jim Bob take care of the watering chores for the baseball practices, and he went up on the mountainside with Gene to cut cedars for corner posts and poplars for crossbeams and for rafters. To the sturdy framework, they would nail the planks they'd brought home from the Slones. They rolled and dragged the logs, one by one, down the mountainside and into the backyard.

Ma stepped off the dimensions of the chicken house, and Gene drove stakes into the four corners. They dug deep holes for the corner posts. Then Gene notched the four cedar trunks and cut two poplar poles, notching them to match the notches on the cedar posts. Ma's chicken house would be tall enough in front for her to enter. It would slope back to a height of four feet, just enough to allow for two rows of nesting boxes.

Gene and Everett set a cedar post into a hole. Ma and Emmy steadied the cedar, while Everett and Dahlia scooped dirt back into the hole and Gene tamped the earth firmly around the post.

Gene urged them to work fast. "We got to get all the posts set and the crossbeams lashed in place before we can leave it," he said. "Even a carefully tamped post won't stand straight without some help."

Dahlia and Emmy supported one end of a poplar pole as Gene fitted its other notched end to the matching notch on the cedar. Using the few extra-long nails Mr. Slone had included in the sack, Gene secured the corners.

"My dad and my uncles back on the farm would have pegged those corners," Ma said. "They didn't believe in nails except for fastening up sideboards or putting on shingles."

Emmy waited for Ma to go on, to tell them how her family had built other things, but Ma turned and went into the house. When she came back carrying the lighted oil lamp, Emmy knew just how excited Ma was about the chicken house. The oil lamp was reserved for emergencies or special occasions

At last the four corners of the house were secured to Gene's satisfaction, and they extinguished the light and went in to bed.

Next afternoon, Emmy took Kate and Marvin to the creek for a little while so Ma could make her pies. Everett and Jim Bob were sitting on the bank. They motioned her and the young ones to stay quiet. The three of them silently sat down beside Everett.

Everett and Jim Bob stared intently at the water. Emmy looked, too. Bubbles rose slowly in the deep pool where she had played a few weeks earlier. Jim Bob and Everett leaned forward. A grin spread over Jim Bob's face, and he started to jump up. But Everett grabbed his arm. "Wait another minute or two," he whispered.

Finally he turned Jim Bob's arm loose. Both boys leaped into the air with a whoop. Then they splashed into the water, waded to the pool, and pulled out their trap. A large turtle was caught in it.

"Turtle soup for supper!" Jim Bob exclaimed, slapping his thigh.

They set the trap on the bank. Kate and Marvin inched

forward. "Don't get too close," Everett warned. "Look." He picked up a stick and poked it into the trap. The turtle lumbered around and then, faster than the blink of an eye, the turtle's head shot out and his jaws clamped on the stick, snapping it in half.

"That's why they call them snapping turtles," Everett told Kate and Marvin. "They can do that to a finger, too, so don't ever fool around with turtles."

Kate looked doubtfully at the creek. "I wanna go home," she said to Emmy.

"It's okay," Emmy said. "I bet Everett and Jim Bob caught the only turtle for miles around." She settled them on a rock to make mud pies.

Emmy sat beside the trap with Everett while Jim Bob ran home to get his wagon. The turtle moved from side to side like a ship rocking on waves. It glared at them with mean-looking eyes. Emmy imagined it would like to snap off all their fingers. But then, she didn't blame it.

Everett did not have pity on his mind. "That turtle shell will bring some money," he said. "I've been studying on what to buy with my part."

"What're you going to get?" Emmy asked.

"Well, I've narrowed it down to two things. I might buy a shotgun so's I can go up on the mountain and get squirrels and rabbits for Ma to cook."

Emmy didn't point out that he'd need to buy shells every time he wanted to go hunting. With not an extra penny in the house, she wasn't sure how often he would get to use the gun.

"But what I want even more is a baseball glove. Then me and Jim Bob could start practicing so someday we'll be good as any player around."

When Jim Bob returned with the wagon, the two boys loaded the heavy trap onto it. The turtle butted against the sides of the trap. "My dad says he'll kill it and divide the meat with your family," Jim Bob said. "Then tomorrow we'll go sell the shell."

Emmy didn't look at the turtle again. Still, that evening when Jim Bob brought over the meat and Ma started browning it in a large skillet, Emmy couldn't help thinking how good the soup was going to taste.

When Gene got home from the mines, he bathed and ate his supper. Then the family went to work once more on the chicken house. They nailed slim poplar poles across the top, forming rafters to which they fastened wood slabs from the Slones' pile, running them perpendicular to the rafters so rain would follow each slab and drip off the back of the chicken house.

Darkness caught them, and they had to stop work before they could begin covering the sides. "We'll get it done when we get it done," Ma said philosophically. But Emmy knew Ma was more eager for the chicken house to be completed than she had been about any family project in a long time.

While Emmy was preparing Kate and Marvin for bed, she heard Pa thrashing about in his bed. She wondered how he could lie in there day after day, hardly speaking to anyone. She thought again of the banjo secreted away in her corner. In all these months, Pa's holding the banjo was as close as he'd come to being himself, to being the pa she had known all her life. She determined to find a way to get the banjo repaired.

Next day, as soon as the dinner dishes were washed and the kitchen clean, Everett went off to find Jim Bob so they could sell the turtle shell. The boarders had been served turtle soup for lunch along with big chunks of cornbread and bowls of coleslaw. They had eaten the soup so fast that Emmy had worried there wouldn't be any left for the family to sample. But Ma knew how to stretch meat. She had cooked up two kettles of the creamy soup, and when the family was ready to eat, she pulled the second kettle from the back of the stove and ladled up seven bowls. "And there's enough left for Gene's supper," she said with satisfaction.

Emmy carried a bowl in to Pa. He didn't acknowledge her or the soup. However, half an hour later when she went back in to check on him, the bowl was empty and Pa was sound asleep. She smiled as she smoothed the sheet over him.

Later, Emmy and Ma were in the garden picking green beans when Petey walked around the house. "Howdy, Mrs. Mourfield," he called. "I don't mean to disturb your work, but I wanted to see that chicken house I been hearing so much about."

Ma led Petey to the partially completed building. Petey put a hand on a corner post and leaned his weight against it. The corner post didn't budge. "I reckon those youngsters of yours are doing a creditable job," he said with a smile.

"I'm right pleased with it myself," Ma said, smiling back at him. "We're beholden to you for the use of your wagon to haul the planks. We'd like to repay you someday. Maybe when our hens begin laying eggs…."

"Now, hold on," Petey said. "You don't owe me a thing. Why, my mules needed a little exercise that day. Besides, your son does such a fine job toting water to the players, I reckon I'm beholden to you for letting me borrow him."

"My son?" Ma looked puzzled.

Emmy drew her breath in sharply.

But Ma was still looking at Petey.

"Everett, I mean," Petey said. "He and Jim Bob are about the best water boys I've found."

Ma recovered quickly from her surprise. "Yes, Everett is a fine worker. I've always been proud of him."

Petey stayed a few minutes longer, asking about the chicken house and inquiring after Pa's health. When he had gone, Ma went back to work. She didn't mention Everett, but Emmy noticed a certain stiffness in her movements that hadn't been there before. Emmy could tell Ma was carefully thinking something out.

Sixteen

THE FAMILY WAS EATING SUPPER when Everett got home. He burst in, full of excitement over selling the turtle shell. "Me and Jim Bob had to walk all the way home from Pikesbury," he said. "That's how come I'm so late. We caught a ride over, but there wasn't anybody coming back."

"Your supper's getting cold," Ma said.

Emmy tried to catch Everett's eye to warn him that Ma knew about his serving as water boy, but Everett was too busy telling about his day to pay attention to anyone else.

"That man who buys the shells sure was glad to get the one we brought him. He said it was the best he'd seen in a long time." Everett reached into the bib of his overalls and pulled out several dollar bills. "And he paid us in cash. No company script that we can only spend at the company store. Nope, he paid us in good old American money." He looked around the table, grinning happily.

"I'll be needing to talk to you in private after supper," Ma said.

"Sure, Ma," Everett answered.

Emmy still hadn't caught his eye to warn him. She gave up with a shrug and went back to eating.

After supper Ma shooed everyone except Everett out of the kitchen. "The rest of you get started on the chicken house," she said. "Everett's going to help me with the dishes."

Everett looked puzzled, but he immediately began clearing the table. "Me and Ma will be through here directly," he said to Gene. "If there's any heavy work left, save it for me."

"I'll go get Pa's dishes," Emmy said, stalling for time to warn Everett.

"Never mind about that," Ma said. "Everett probably wants to tell Pa about the turtle shell. He can get the dishes."

Emmy followed Gene, Dahlia, Kate, and Marvin to the backyard, leaving Everett whistling between his teeth as he headed for Pa's room. She soon put Everett out of her mind as she began helping with the building project.

First they cut the poplar saplings into lengths, notched them, and secured them in place. Because the saplings were light, Emmy and Dahlia were able to help Gene with them. Still, Gene glanced frequently at the back door, and Emmy knew he would be as glad as she would be to see Everett come through the doorway—although for different reasons.

Finally, Ma and Everett came outside together. Ma was her usual self, pitching in to get all the sills and beams in place before dark. Everett, however, was much quieter than when he had burst in during supper.

When Gene sent Everett to the mountainside to find one more sapling to serve as a cross support, Emmy volunteered to go with him. "Get a skinny one," Gene said. "The two of you ought to be able to carry it together."

Everett picked up the hatchet, and Emmy followed him across the yard and through the gate.

"What did Ma say?" she asked when she caught up with him.

Everett grinned ruefully. "She found out about the baseball games."

"Petey's visit," Emmy said with a nod. "I knew that was

going to mean trouble. I tried to warn you at supper, but you wouldn't look at me."

"It wouldn't have mattered. I reckon once Ma knew I'd been deceitful, there wasn't any way for me to miss a tongue-lashing."

"Was a tongue-lashing all you got?"

"Well, you know Ma doesn't give lickings." Then Everett laughed. "I guess if Pa hadn't been laid up in bed, he would have given me a good one." He looked thoughtful again. "'Course, Ma came up with her own punishment."

"What did she do?"

"She told me I wasn't the team's water boy anymore."

Everett kicked at a clump of moist leaves, releasing a whiff of air that filled Emmy's nostrils with the good earth smell she associated with Ma's garden. She wasn't surprised at the punishment Ma had decided on. Ma always said the punishment ought to fit the crime.

Then she thought of her own crime. "Does Ma know I went to a game with you?" she asked.

"Naw, I didn't tell her." Everett grinned again. Emmy was always surprised at Everett's good humor, even when he was in trouble. "She didn't ask any questions. She just told me what she'd found out. Then she gave me a talk about honesty."

Everett picked out a proper-sized sapling and felled it with several swift blows from the hatchet. He resumed his story as he and Emmy dragged the sapling down the mountainside. "Ma said she would have been proud for me to be water boy if I'd just come and told her about it to start with. But she said she doesn't hold with lying and sneaking, and I'd better learn right away that I can't get by with such carryings-on."

Emmy could hear Ma saying all those things. Everett had known from the time he slipped off to the first game that even though there was a chance Ma might not give her approval to his being water boy, it was a sure thing she wouldn't approve if he sneaked around to do it. Still, Everett had decided not to risk asking, gambling she'd never find out. And that was like him, Emmy concluded. Life was more exciting for Everett if he could add an element of danger to whatever he was doing.

BUT EMMY DIDN'T LIVE WELL WITH DANGER. Nor with guilt. For the next week she stewed over her getting away with sneaking out to the ball game. Along with that worry, she was still trying to figure out how to get Pa's banjo repaired. She finally had an idea about the banjo, but she needed Ma's permission.

One afternoon while she was in the garden with Ma, she said, "You know, I think if Pa could learn to play his banjo again, he might want to come out of his room."

Ma looked hard at Emmy. "I wouldn't pin too many hopes on that," she said. Then she shook her head. "Still, anything is worth a try. But I thought the banjo was broken."

"It is. But I kept it. And Mr. Slone offered to fix it."

"Well, I reckon we're already too beholden to Mr. Slone," Ma said with a nod toward the chicken house.

"But I've got an idea how to pay him," Emmy said.

Ma stopped weeding.

"His office is an awful mess, dusty and with windows so dirty you can't see through them. I thought I'd offer to clean in exchange for a new back for Pa's banjo."

"Well, now I don't know but what I like that idea. There's nothing wrong with a little hard work, but you'll have to get Everett to go over with you. I can't have you alone at that lumberyard."

Emmy thought of kindly Mr. Slone and his sons, who acted so much like her own brothers. She couldn't see any danger in being there. Still, she was glad Ma had agreed so readily, even if she did attach one condition. Emmy was sure Everett would be glad to go with her.

She was right. Now that he couldn't be water boy, Everett had no way to get to the baseball games out of town. On those days, he was at loose ends without Jim Bob around. So on Saturday morning, Emmy got the banjo out of the corner, and she and Everett walked to the Slones'.

On the way, she asked Everett how he'd decided to spend the money he got from the turtle shell. "Well, I reckon that's going to be a surprise," he said. "I decided to get something all the family will get some use out of."

"If the whole family can use it, I don't guess you're getting the baseball mitt," Emmy said.

"Nope."

"The gun?"

"Nope."

No matter how much Emmy pleaded, Everett wouldn't tell her what he was going to buy. "You'll just have to wait and be surprised, too," he said.

Mr. Slone was delighted with Emmy's offer to clean. "My Hattie used to come down here and clean for me once in a while. But when she saw me and the boys didn't make any effort to keep the place straight after she'd worked so hard, she said she had better things to do with her time."

Emmy handed him the banjo.

He strummed it appreciatively. "A fine instrument," he said with a nod. Then he examined the back. "I can replace that easy enough. 'Course, you know it'll take me a few days. Can you come back for it about the middle of next week?"

"Yes, sir," Emmy said. Looking around the shed she thought she might still be there cleaning until the middle of the week, but Everett pitched in and helped her. The two of them unpiled the desk and dusted its surface. Then they stacked all the papers back on it neatly. They cleaned the shelves, one by one, so they didn't get any of the supplies out of order.

"If I had some stove black, I could really make this shine," Everett said as he dusted the potbelly stove in the middle of the room.

At dinnertime, Mrs. Slone brought them a basket containing fluffy biscuits, each of which had a slice of ham in it. A jar of milk, two pieces of apple pie, and some boiled eggs rounded out the basket lunch.

Everett looked at the boiled eggs and broke into a grin. "Right under my nose," he said. "Mrs. Slone, would you happen to have any laying hens you'd be willing to sell?"

Emmy looked at him in surprise. So *that* was what he was going to spend his money on. There was never any figuring out Everett.

"I might have," Mrs. Slone said. She ran a hand over the desk. "I don't know how you two managed to bring order to this mess," she said.

"I sure would like to buy a few hens from you," Everett persisted.

Mrs. Slone stopped examining the room and rubbed her nose. "Let me see now, those young biddies that hatched out this spring have done right well. No possums or weasels got them yet. Yes, I could let you have a few from that lot."

Everett looked jubilant. "I've got enough money to buy several, if you don't want too much."

"I don't usually sell biddies—just eggs and old hens ready for the pot. I don't hardly know how to price biddies." Mrs. Slone stepped to the doorway and looked toward the house. "But seeing all this good work you youngsters have done gives me an idea." She motioned for Everett and Emmy to join her. "Now if I charged you cash for those young hens, I'd just spend the money on some kind of foolishness—a new hat or something I'd have to dust." She laughed. "Lord knows, I don't need any more of that. So, how would you like to work out the price of the biddies?"

"If Ma can spare me long enough, I'd like that just fine," Everett said. "What did you have in mind?"

"Well, I think it's kind of nice the way the sunlight comes in these clean windows. Would you be willing to help me wash the windows in that old house?" She pointed toward their house, a two-story wood-frame structure built by Mr. Slone. And in building he hadn't spared the windows.

"I reckon I can handle it," said Everett.

Mrs. Slone held out her hand. "It's a deal then. When you come back for the banjo, we'll wash windows. You can fetch the biddies at the same time."

Everett shook her hand. "That ought to just about give us time to finish boarding up the chicken house."

He couldn't stop grinning after Mrs. Slone left. "Now I can give Ma her chickens and still get the baseball mitt."

Emmy felt as good as Everett, not as if she'd worked hard all morning. "Everything's working out just right for us now, isn't it?" she asked.

With their energy replenished by the dinner, Emmy and Everett went back to their cleaning. They were almost through when a sharp sound pierced the quiet afternoon. The mine whistle!

Seventeen

EMMY AND EVERETT DASHED out of the lumber office. Mrs. Slone was running out of the house.

"We have to go, ma'am," Everett yelled.

"Wait," Mrs. Slone called back. "We'll take you in the wagon."

As she spoke, Mr. Slone and the two boys pulled into the lumberyard, a load of logs behind them. The boys jumped down and began unhitching the mules.

Mr. Slone hurried over to Everett and Emmy. "Is Gene...?"

Emmy and Everett nodded.

"We'll all go," Mr. Slone said briskly.

Willard and Albert led the mules to an empty wagon, and within a few minutes the team was hitched and ready to go. Mrs. Slone had disappeared into the house after she spoke to Emmy and Everett, and now she reappeared carrying a basket.

"It'll be a long evening," she said as she set the basket on the wagon bed.

"You sit up front," Albert said. He helped her up to the wagon seat. Then he and Willard jumped onto the wagon with Emmy and Everett. Mr. Slone slapped the reins across the mules' backs, and the wagon rolled away from the lumberyard.

The whistle continued its piercing wail. Everett squeezed Emmy's hand. His touch was reassuring, and Emmy was glad he was there with her. Still, she couldn't stop the pounding of her heart nor the way the coppery taste of fear filled her mouth.

Her fear was as acute as it had been last winter when the mine whistle had blown in late afternoon, and had gone on blowing and blowing, announcing a mine accident—the accident that had crippled Pa. That day she had come in from school and sat at the large table in the kitchen, the table the boarders now used for their dinners. Ma was cooking supper for the eight of them. Kate and Marvin played on the floor. Emmy had spread out her books and started her homework, feeling content that afternoon, secure in the small miner's house surrounded by her family. The sound of the mine whistle had destroyed more than her mood; the accident it had shrilled to the world had come close to destroying her family.

And now on this summer afternoon the whistle was blowing again. She returned the pressure of Everett's grip as they bounced in the wagon over the rough road.

Mr. Slone flicked the reins on the mules' backs, urging them on, although they were already running so fast that foam had formed around the bits in their mouths and blew back along their necks.

When they reached the edge of town, Mr. Slone allowed the mules to slow a bit. There was no one in sight. They passed the first few houses, then the Mourfields' house. Emmy looked at her home briefly, but she didn't see anyone. Was Pa still inside, lying in his bed, listening to the whistle?

A few minutes later, they turned up the hollow leading to the tipple. To their left the town square lay quiet and deserted. Not until they rounded a curve and the tipple came into view did they see anyone. All of town had gathered at the head of the hollow.

Mr. Slone stopped the mules at the edge of the crowd. Emmy and Everett jumped from the wagon and pushed their way through the people. Here and there a miner covered with coal dust stood with his family.

As she and Everett hurried past, Emmy searched each blackened face, but she knew if Gene were out of the mine, he would be with Ma, Dahlia, and the little ones.

"Jim Bob," Everett called when he saw the Halls.

Jim Bob and Nick turned together.

"Where's Ma?" Everett asked.

"Your family's over near the tipple entrance," Nick said.

"Is Gene...?" Emmy began. She couldn't finish her question.

Nick Hall put a hand on her arm. "Gene hasn't come out yet, and we don't know anything for sure about the men who are still down there."

Emmy nodded numbly.

"I'll take you to your family," Nick said.

Emmy and Everett followed Nick as he made his way through the crowds. People moved aside readily for him. Everett was still gripping Emmy by the hand, and she realized Jim Bob had taken her other hand. She felt as if her body had no life left in it, as if it were those two hands that kept her blood flowing.

"Here's Emmy and Everett," she heard Nick say. Then he stepped aside.

"Pa!" Everett yelled.

Emmy looked into Pa's face. She swayed toward Pa, the feeling that the world had gone crazy about to swallow her— Gene trapped in the mines, Pa out of bed.

Pa dropped the big stick he was using as a cane. He hugged Emmy to his chest. Emmy wasn't sure if she was holding up Pa or if he was keeping her from falling. They clung to each other. Everett had his arm around Ma, and Dahlia hugged Kate and Marvin to her. For a long moment they looked at one another, none of them daring to speak.

Emmy finally found her voice. "Pa, how did you get here?" she asked.

"The neighbors," Pa said. "When I heard the whistle, I knew Gene was up here…Gene and lots of other men…my friends."

"I was in the garden when the whistle blew," Ma said. "I ran inside and your pa was coming out of the bedroom, leaning on a chair. Marvin and Kate were crying…."

Pa tightened his arm around Emmy. "With your ma's help, I got out the door and down the steps. I picked up this stick…."

"We had just started up the road," Ma continued, "me carrying Marvin, Kate helping Pa as best she could. Then Dahlia came running and took Marvin, so I could help Pa."

"The Bradfords came along," Pa said, "and a couple of other neighbors. I couldn't hardly make it and was wearing your ma out. But Tom Bradford and Joe Jenkins made a pack-saddle out of their arms…"

Emmy nodded. She and her friends sometimes made pack-saddles—folded their hands and arms into seats to carry one another in their games.

Ma looked toward the mine entrance. "We made it up here, but we haven't been able to find out a thing since we got here."

"There's no word from the trapped men…." Pa couldn't continue. Tears slid down his cheeks.

Even in all the pain from his accident, Emmy had never seen Pa cry. He had been quarrelsome and depressed, and had shut them out. But he had never cried…until now with Gene trapped in the mine.

"Why don't you sit down awhile, Pa?" she said.

Everett supported Pa on the left, and the two of them led him to a large rock and helped him sit down.

Pa began talking. "When I heard the whistle, I knew

Gene was still underground. I could feel the roof falling the way it did that day…one timber giving way, then another… the slate falling all around me…that large piece pinning me." Pa stopped. "Only this time it was falling on my son," he said.

"Is that what happened today, Pa? Did the roof fall?" Emmy asked.

Pa shook his head and looked at her. "I don't know….I just don't know."

"Thank the Lord, you both got here," Ma said, laying a hand on Emmy's shoulder.

"We heard the whistle all the way in Hawkins Branch," Everett said.

"The Slones brought us," Emmy added. She looked around and saw Mr. and Mrs. Slone making their way toward them.

Pa pushed himself back up onto his good leg and held his right hand out to Mr. Slone. "We're mighty beholden to you," he said.

"None of that," Mr. Slone said gruffly, gripping Pa's hand. "We would have come anyway."

Then Nick Hall was standing beside them. "I've talked to the mining officials," he said.

"Tell us…," Ma began.

"What's happened?" Pa asked.

"They aren't sure," Nick said, "but they know there was an explosion. The miners near the front got out, but twenty-three of them were working way back in the mine."

Emmy didn't want to hear what he would say next, but she couldn't make herself turn away.

"Those men are still in there," Nick continued, "and Gene's one of them. They're all trapped."

"How bad is it? Do they know…Are the trapped men…?" Ma couldn't go on.

Mrs. Slone put an arm around Ma.

"They're hoping they're all alive," Nick said.

Pa nodded. "But they got to get them out of there before the air is gone!"

"They're working right now to do that," Nick said. He turned to Everett. "Some of the women have made a kettle of coffee. Why don't you get your family some?"

Everett left with Nick. Emmy wanted to comfort Pa, but there was nothing comforting to say. Pa knew better than she did the danger of being in a mine during an explosion.

Ma stood straight as the poplar poles they'd felled on the mountainside, her arms by her side, hands clenched. "Dahlia, you take Kate and Marvin back to the house," she said. "No need to keep them out here."

"Pa, why don't you sit back down. And you, too, Ma," Emmy said when Dahlia, Kate, and Marvin had gone, Mrs. Slone helping by carrying Marvin.

"You watch out for your pa. I got to see what's going on," Ma said. She turned toward the mine entrance, shading her eyes with her hand.

Emmy looked, too, but there was nothing to see—just more families huddled together waiting.

In a few minutes Everett was back. "Here, Ma, drink this," he said, handing her a cup of coffee. He handed another cup to Pa. "I'll get us some, too," he said to Emmy, and left again.

Emmy wanted to call after him to tell him she didn't want coffee, but she just stood and watched him go.

When he gave Emmy her cup, she put her mouth against the heavy crockery and sucked in some of the steaming liquid. It was bitter, so bitter she almost spat it out. She drank coffee at home—even Kate was given a cup when she wanted it. But their coffee was always mostly milk. In the winter Ma would heat the milk, so that as they drank the pale mixture they were warmed through and through. Now she held the black coffee in her mouth for a moment, its heat cutting into the roof of her mouth. Finally, eyes stinging, she swallowed it.

Suddenly there was a stirring among the people nearest the mine opening—a movement that spread through the crowd like a wind blowing through a wooded area.

"They've got through to them," someone shouted.

Ma started forward. Pa tried to get up to follow her. Ma laid a hand on his shoulder. "It'll be a while before they get them out, Frank," she said. "You just rest here, and I'll let you know what's happening."

But Pa wouldn't sit back down. "I got to know," he said.

"I'll help you, Pa," Everett said, slipping an arm around Pa.

Emmy looked at Everett holding Pa up and making room for all of them along the rope strung around the mine opening. She supposed with Gene trapped in the mine and Pa disabled, Everett was head of the family. But she couldn't let herself think about that. Gene was going to be all right— he had to be all right.

Mr. Dowdy came out of the mine entrance.

"What's happened to the men?" someone called.

"Let us through. We got husbands and sons...."

Mr. Dowdy held up his hand. The crowd fell silent. "The rescue workers have broken through the rock slide," he said. "They've got air in to the men now, and they're working on making an opening to bring them out. But it's going to take a few more hours."

Moans rose from the crowd.

"I know how you feel," Mr. Dowdy said. "But they're doing everything possible." He turned and walked into the tipple office.

"Come on, Pa," Everett said. "Let's go back and sit down. There's nothing we can do here."

In a few minutes, Mrs. Slone came to them, carrying the basket she'd put on the wagon. "It's not much," she said. "There wasn't time...." She bent over the basket and took out plates of sliced ham and biscuits. Then she set out a pie and sliced it, the smell of sweetened apples and cinnamon drifting in the air.

Ma and Pa looked at the food as if it were something from another world.

Mrs. Slone nodded to them. "It doesn't seem like the time for food," she said. "But you need to eat, need to keep your strength up." She handed the food around, and the four Mourfields ate, swallowing the food, scarcely tasting it.

Mrs. Slone passed some extra food around to the families gathered nearby. A few had cold cornbread or other food a family member had gone home and gotten, but most had nothing and were grateful for the little left from Mrs. Slone's basket.

Time dragged on. Occasionally, one of the men Pa had worked with in the mines stopped to speak to him. Pa nodded to each but didn't enter into conversation.

Mr. Dowdy passed through the crowd, reassuring those who stopped him. He spent a few minutes with Pa until Tennie came looking for her father. Mr. Dowdy rose, shook Pa's hand, and followed Tennie back toward the tipple area.

Emmy hoped that something was happening. Maybe someone was reaching the trapped men in the mine shaft. But no announcements were made.

Priscilla came by with a bucket of water. She gave some to Pa and Ma, then handed a cup to Emmy. They all mumbled their thanks.

"I'm sorry...." Priscilla didn't seem to know what to say, but she looked genuinely concerned.

"Thank you," Emmy said again.

Priscilla looked around. "Dahlia…?"

"Ma sent her home with the little ones," Emmy said.

"Will you tell her for me…tell her I'm sorry." Priscilla picked up her bucket and hurried away.

Suddenly there was a commotion at the mouth of the mine.

"They're bringing them out," someone shouted.

With Everett helping Pa again, they moved to the front of the crowd. The people who had family members still underground were given the front positions along the rope.

A company official shouted above the noise, "We can't get them out if you get in the way."

The pushing stopped.

"We'll call the name as we bring the miner out," the official continued.

When the crowd grew quiet, the official said, "We'll be taking the injured to the tipple office. Family members can join them there."

"And what about the dead?" someone muttered.

If the official heard, he gave no indication.

"Henry McIntyre." The first name rang out, and a family passed beyond the rope and walked toward the mining office. Four men carried a stretcher from the mine's entrance to the office.

Six more names were called. Two of the men were on stretchers, but four of them walked out, supported by rescue workers. Their families cried out in relief.

Emmy counted off men as the names were called—seven of the twenty-three out now, sixteen left. The list of names went on, as more men came out, some walking, some on stretchers. Finally there were only two names uncalled. Were they waiting to bring out the worst injured last? No, that wouldn't make any sense.

"Gene Mourfield."

"Thank God!" Ma cried as she, Emmy, Everett, and Pa strained forward.

Gene walked out of the mine without anyone helping him and stood blinking in the sunlight.

Eighteen

THERE HAD BEEN NO FATALITIES IN THIS ACCIDENT, but several men were being treated by the company doctor while they waited for a train to take them to the nearest hospital, a four- or five-hour ride away. There the men would stay, far from their families, until they were able to return home.

After repeatedly assuring the family that he was not hurt, Gene helped them get Pa home. On the way they met Dahlia, Kate, and Marvin. Dahlia ran to hug Gene, dirty as he was. Emmy felt tears well up behind her eyelids. She wiped a hand across her eyes and scooped Marvin up in her arms.

When they reached the house, Ma helped Pa back to bed. By the time she had pulled the covers up over him, he was asleep.

Gene scrubbed himself on the back porch. Emmy wanted to ask him about the accident, but she was afraid to bring it up.

When Gene had washed away the coal dust, they all sat around the dining table and ate bowls of beans and cornbread Dahlia had cooked. Ma just picked at her food, unable to take her eyes off Gene, who was eating hungrily. Finally he scraped the last bite of beans from his bowl, pushed back his chair, and looked around at all of them. Now he was ready to talk.

"We heard the explosion from someplace off in the mine," he said. "It wasn't very loud, just a distant roar. But all the men knew what it meant. 'Let's get out of here,' they said. We dropped our drills and picks, and we started back up the passage.

"We came maybe a quarter of a mile—we're working a seam pretty far back—and we saw a cave-in. The roof had fallen. The explosion probably jarred a rock loose.

"We came flat up against rock and coal just piled up where it used to be an open passageway. There wasn't any way around it. The whole roof was down."

Ma's face was paler than ever, as if she still didn't believe Gene had gotten out.

"I guess most of us looked pretty grim about then. We didn't see any way out," Gene repeated. "Then one man— name of Fain—sort of took charge. 'I been in worse spots,' he said. 'We'll get out of this if we just stay calm.'

"He sent pairs of men off to search some of the other hallways, to see if there was a way out and to see if any men had been hurt. They all came back, some of them carrying men, some of them leading men. But nobody had found a way out.

"'Looks like we'll have to wait for help,' Fain said. Then he had us turn off our lights. 'It'll be dark,' he warned us. But there wasn't no need to burn up oxygen with the lights, so we all put them out. And it *was* dark, the darkest I've ever seen, so dark it made your eyes ache to have them open, you wanted that bad to see something through the darkness."

Emmy closed her eyes. She could still see the shapes of her family gathered around the table. The darkness was a red-brown, not the black she imagined underground must be. Sometimes on moonless nights she awoke to a dark house, but even then she could make out Dahlia and Kate in bed with her, their silhouettes darker than the surrounding night. She wondered what it would be like not to be able to see anything at all, even with her eyes wide open.

"All we could do was wait," Gene went on. "Some of the men were praying out loud. Some of them, I think, were crying, just a snuffle now and then. Then somebody started singing a hymn. One by one, we all joined in. Somehow the darkness didn't look so black with all the voices around, and from time to time it was like I could see those voices, not just hear them.

"Every once in a while, we'd stop singing to listen. Fain said the rescuers would be coming for us most anytime now."

Gene rubbed a hand over his face. "I wanted to believe him, but there were times I had trouble thinking anybody even knew we were down there. It sure seemed like forever. Right toward the end, some of the men started to cough. I knew what was happening. The oxygen was beginning to give out. Them that had weaker lungs were suffering before us younger ones. But I knew it'd come to all of us soon if we didn't get out."

Ma looked away from Gene toward the kitchen and the door to Pa's room.

Gene seemed to know what she was thinking. "But we did get out," he said in a soft voice. "Fain was right. We heard noises from beyond the rock fall, and we knew the rescuers were cutting their way through the cave-in. Fain tapped them a message, and I reckon they heard it because they started drilling on that rock pile. Fresh air started coming in the holes they made—and just in time. Those of us who were doing all right had them take the others out first. It was a long wait, but the smell of that fresh air as I walked up that mine shaft was about the sweetest I expect to ever smell. You know the rest."

Gene stood and stretched. "I reckon I'm pretty tired."

"You get on to bed," Ma said. "All of you," she added, looking around the table.

Marvin had fallen asleep, his head on the table. Emmy went around the table to pick him up, but Dahlia reached him first. Dahlia lifted him, smiling at Emmy over Marvin's limp body. Emmy smiled back. Later, as she fell asleep, Kate's warm body in the crook of her arm, Emmy hoped Priscilla and Dahlia would make up.

THE MINE WAS CLOSED for a few days while the fallen rock was removed. Several company officials rode in on a train and spent time down in the mine inspecting. They also talked to all the miners who had been trapped.

"It's because of the union," Gene told his family. "The union is threatening to come close them down, and the company is scared." He grinned. "The men say they haven't ever seen the company scared of anything before."

Despite his cheer, he was out of work for those two days, and there would be no pay for the missed time. Emmy thought it wasn't fair that the miners were the losers all the way around, but she supposed getting the mine safe again was worth missing the money.

When he wasn't talking to the company officials or the other miners, Gene spent his time working on the chicken house. Ma had extra cooking to do—some of the visiting officials ate at her table—and Emmy, Everett, and Dahlia helped her.

By the time Gene returned to the mines, the chicken house was completely covered with boards, and he had fashioned a door, making the hinges of leather.

It was Saturday before Ma could spare Emmy to go back to the Slones' to pick up the banjo. Ma gathered a bouquet of cosmos and zinnias to send to Mrs. Slone—"To thank her for her kindness," Ma said. And she asked Everett once more to go with Emmy.

"If Mr. Slone's got any work for us to do, we'll stay and do that," he said.

They borrowed Mrs. Bradford's chicken crate and Jim Bob's wagon. Ma didn't know what they were up to, but Emmy didn't feel guilty about the deception. She was happy to be heading for the Slones', eager to surprise Ma with the hens.

She wished she could be sure about Pa's reaction to the banjo. The day of the mine accident had so tired him that he had slept most of the week. He seemed to save his strength for seeing Gene each evening when he got off from work.

Mrs. Slone was glad to have the flowers and delighted to see Emmy and Everett. And when Emmy volunteered to help wash the windows, Mrs. Slone said, "I declare. I didn't bargain for two workers. I guess I'll throw in two more biddies."

With three of them working, the chore took only a couple of hours. Then, while Everett and Mrs. Slone caught the chickens, Emmy went to find Mr. Slone.

He was sitting in the shed, the banjo across his lap. "The boys told me Hattie had you two hard at work again," he said.

Emmy nodded. She looked quickly around the office. It seemed still to be clean.

Mr. Slone laughed. "In good weather, me and the boys don't have time to mess it up in here." Then he looked more serious. "How are your pa and Gene?"

Emmy assured him her family was well, and he handed her the banjo. "Here's your pa's banjo, good as new, I hope."

Emmy ran her hand over the back. The wood was as smooth and mellow as the wood on any of the instruments hanging on Mr. Slone's wall. He had more than kept his end of the bargain.

"It's even better than new," she said. "Pa will be pleased."

But as she and Everett walked home, pulling the wagon loaded with the crate of chickens, she wondered if Pa really would be pleased. Or would he just throw the banjo on the floor again?

There was no doubt about Ma's pleasure. Emmy and Everett had planned to slip around to the back and put the hens in the house, but Ma was sitting on the porch when they came down the road. As they pulled their load into the yard, she came down the steps.

Tears slipped silently down Ma's face when she saw the chickens.

Emmy didn't know whether to pat Ma on the arm or to pretend she didn't see the tears. Everett just grinned and pulled the wagon around to the backyard.

Emmy and Ma followed. They lifted the biddies, one by one, from the crate and put them in the chicken house. Emmy liked the feel of the feathery hens and the firmness of their wings folded against their bodies. She liked the way they moved their small heads from side to side, looking over their new surroundings. She even liked the faint ammonia smell the crate had taken on.

Ma set out a pan of water and scattered some dried corn around on the dirt floor. "We'll keep them closed up for a few days till they learn the place," she said happily.

WHILE THEY WERE EATING DINNER in the kitchen, Nick Hall came by to see Pa. After he left, they heard Pa moving around in the bedroom. Ma glanced at the door occasionally, but went on eating. Although hungry from her morning of work and walking, Emmy paid little attention to the food she put in her mouth. She could think only of the banjo, which she had left on the sofa before dinner.

Suddenly Ma dropped her fork. Emmy quickly swung around on the bench.

Pa stood in the doorway wearing a pair of old overalls that hung loosely from his lean shoulders.

"Frank..." Ma began, rising from the table.

"Sit down, Sally," Pa said. "I thought I'd have dinner with my young'uns." He smiled and leaned against the doorjamb.

Everett rushed to the sitting room and brought back a chair for Pa. Emmy rose to help Pa, but he waved her away and made his way to the table with the help of a large stick.

When Dahlia started to fill a plate, Pa stopped her. "Just a bite or two," he said. She spooned up a small amount of corn and green beans and put a biscuit on the side. Pa nodded.

When Pa had eaten a little, he laid down his fork and pushed back from the table. "I'm aiming to go out this evening," he said.

"Where?" asked Ma.

"There's a union meeting," Pa said.

"But how...?" Ma stopped and looked down at her hands.

"Nick said Petey was planning to bring his wagon around. Seems like some other crippled"—he looked around at them and said in a firm voice—"other miners who've been hurt are going to this meeting, too."

He stood, wobbling slightly as he rested on the stick. "And working miners are going. Gene said he's aiming to go, too."

Ma sighed. "Even if Gene loses his job because of union activities, that's nowhere near as bad as his losing his life because of no union."

Pa turned toward the sitting room. "I reckon I'll sit a spell on the porch."

As he crossed the kitchen and went into the sitting room, his walking played a tune in Emmy's ears—the clump of his heavy shoe, followed by the tap of the stick and the soft shuffle of his other foot. Then sound stopped.

"'Scuse me," Emmy said. She slipped quickly from the bench and hurried into the sitting room.

Pa was staring at the banjo, and he looked at Emmy when she entered the room. "I thought I told you to get rid of that," he said, nodding toward the sofa.

"You did, Pa."

Emmy ran around her father and picked up the banjo, pressing it to her chest. Her heart was beating so hard that she expected to hear the banjo echo its thumping.

Pa sank into a chair.

Emmy let out her breath. "Pa, I'm sorry I went against what you told me," she said, turning the banjo over in her arms and stroking its new back. "I just couldn't throw it away...."

Pa looked up at Emmy, anger draining from his face. He laid his stick on the floor and motioned for her to come to him.

When she placed the banjo on his lap, he ran his hand over the back. "Sure is pretty," he said. Then a small smile tugged at the corners of his mouth. "I guess you got more than your share of the Mourfield stubbornness," he said. "Do you reckon you got enough to learn banjo from your one-armed pa?"

Emmy wasn't sure she'd ever learn to play the banjo, to strum it the way Pa used to, music pouring out of it like a river. But even if she never became a real banjo player, she could learn some, at least enough to play along while the family sang. She smiled back at Pa. "I guess I got your blood aplenty, Pa," she said.

"Take care of this." Pa handed the banjo to Emmy. He went out to the porch and Emmy heard the swing creak under his weight. She hugged the banjo once more.

Someday, between her and Pa, they would fill the house with the cheerful, toe-tapping music of Pa's banjo.

Connie Jordan Green grew up in Oak Ridge, the setting for her first young people's novel, *The War at Home*. Her second novel, *Emmy*, is set in Southeastern Kentucky where many of her relatives live. Both novels were published by Margaret McElderry Books, Macmillan, now Simon & Schuster. The novels have received various awards: *The War at Home* was placed on the ALA List of Best Books for Young Adults, both books were selected by the New York City Library as Books for the Teen Age, *The War at Home* was nominated to the 1991-92 Volunteer State Book Award Master List, and *Emmy* was selected as a Notable 1992 Children's Trade Book in the Field of Social Studies. She also writes poetry, short stories for young people, and a weekly newspaper column that has run since 1978 in *The Loudon County News Herald*. Her poetry and essays have been published in numerous journals and anthologies, including a novel excerpt in *Listen Here: Women Writing in Appalachia*, a landmark collection of literature by Appalachian women. She teaches writing at various workshops, and she speaks frequently at both middle and high schools. She lives on a farm in Loudon County with her husband, a retired engineer. They have three grown children and seven grandchildren.

CPSIA information can be obtained at www.ICGtesting.com
Printed in the USA
LVOW072141080212

267781LV00001B/274/P